MW00978609

Dudes Take Over

BOOK TWO:
The Dudes Adventure Chronicles

By **Tyler Reynolds**
and **Emily Kay Johnson**

Epic Spiel Press

Epic Spiel Press

To all the school teachers and staff I've known...and who are NOT depicted in this book!

To some impossible Dudes: Owen, Lincoln, Aidan, Asher, and Kai

And to Chloe, Sufyana, and Aydina, who can and do put Dudes in their place.

The Dudes Adventure Chronicles:

Save the Dudes

Dudes Take Over

Table of Contents

 *Prologue*

This is Book Two of the Dudes Adventure Chronicles. (I tell you that up front, so you don't have to wonder where you are in the story.)

If you've been reading the Chronicles so far, you know all about me: Tyler Reynolds, and my four friends: Ryan, Connor, Nate, and Deven. We call ourselves the Dudes, which adults sometimes think is weird. Not that we care what they think. After all, they were wrong last summer when they tried to break us up and send Nate to private school.

Last summer we: used ninja stealth to evade the police, demolished the school playground, got arrested by superheroes, and raised a zombie hoard. Oh yeah, and we saved Nate from the fate to which his brilliance had doomed him. I wrote about it all so that future generations would come to know the story of our awesomeness.

If you haven't read Book One, you might be thinking that this is a story about troublemakers. But, believe me, the Dudes are upstanding citizens of Sherwood Heights. In fact, we're a lot more mature and responsible than the grown-ups think. Sometimes we even take over for them.

But don't take my word for it. Judge for yourself in the adventures that follow...

Dudes Together

It was the morning of the first day of school, and the Dudes were together again—well, almost. Deven and Nate and I were early. Nate's always early, which is lucky because he often has to run home again to get stuff he's forgotten. Deven was early because his sister dropped him off on her way to orchestra practice at the high school.

And I was early because it was my brother Jayden's first day of kindergarten. He was so excited that he ran the whole way when I had planned enough time for dragging him.

"That's my big brother, Tyler," I heard him tell the other kids when I dumped him at the kindergarten door. "He's a Dude!"

Their spooky little-kid eyes followed me as I escaped around the corner of the building.

I joined Deven and Nate outside the fifth-grade door.

"I wish it was still summer," said Nate.

"I wish there was no school," I said.

"I don't," Deven said. "If I didn't have school, I would probably have to practice piano all day." He glared at his fingers.

"Mom signed me up for lessons just like Shaila used to have," he explained. (Shaila is his sister.) "Mom says when I've practiced one hundred minutes I get to go to a movie."

"What are you going to see?" I asked.

Deven shrugged and answered, "Whatever is out in 2029, I guess."

Nate and I laughed. Deven could pretty much always make us laugh.

"I wish the Dudes were in the same class this year," I said.

It wasn't gonna happen, though. For one thing, Connor and Ryan can't be in the same class because they're twins—not the identical kind—and their mom wants them to "develop their own talents". I guess she means talents that don't involve bickering or brawling because they do that best together.

The rest of us are split up too. Nate and Deven are in Mr Isaak's class. Connor has the new teacher, Ms Finch. And I'm in Mrs. Hancock's class with Ryan, which is unlucky because Mrs. Hancock is really old and strict. But it's lucky too because Ryan is the leader of the Dudes, so I'll get the first chance to hear all his cool plans.

Speaking of cool, I could see Ryan and Connor coming now, walking on the sidewalk beside their dad who was coasting along the school driveway on his motorcycle.

Ryan and Connor's parents split up last year. Their dad got a new apartment in town and a new job as a math professor at the community college. Now Ryan and Connor would be spending every other weekend with him. It would cut into Dude time, of course, but Dad time is pretty important too.

Mr. Maguire parked at the curb and swung his leg over to walk the guys up to the door. For a parent, Mr. Maguire was cool. For one thing, there was his motorcycle. Sure, it allowed him to ride in the carpool lane and park close to his office. But it also gave him an excuse to wear a leather jacket and motorcycle boots.

"Look, Dad!" shouted Connor, walking the top of the bike rack like a tight-rope. (When he didn't fall off things and get injured, Connor was a real acrobat.)

Mr. Maguire raised a thumbs-up to Connor. Then he gave us each a high five.

"Fifth-graders! Ready to take over the school?" he asked. He struck a casual pose with his hands in the pockets of his jacket.

I noticed Ryan and Connor doing the same thing. I tried to loosen my shoulders too. Nate stood straight and stiff as always. And Deven leaned back a little too casually and bonked his head against the brick wall.

"I remember when my friends and I were in fifth-grade," said Mr. Maguire. He smiled like he was seeing himself all the way back then—probably an eleven-year-old in a leather jacket. "We were the kings of cool," he told us.

Another cool thing about Mr. Maguire: he

grew up right here in Sherwood Heights and even went to school at Sherwood Elementary. Sometimes he told stories about the old days--like how they used to have a real Sammy the Seal mascot, a live seal, in a long tank in the lunchroom. (Sort of like when they have lobsters in a restaurant, I guess.)

Anyway, he said one time, a long time ago, somebody brought their bb gun to school, and it went off in the lunchroom and the kid got expelled and his bb gun got confiscated. No one got hurt, so nobody thought to look for the bb. But, the thing is, it had ricocheted and cracked the back panel of the seal tank. Mr. Maguire said nobody noticed the slow leak it caused, but the tank drained overnight and Sammy died!

Mr. Maguire says that's why we can't bring guns to school—even toys. I figure it's also why we don't have a live mascot but only a plush seal doll in the trophy case.

Of course, Nate had questioned some of the facts of the case. Among other things, he pointed out that, being a mammal, a seal can breathe air and should have been able to survive out of water overnight.

I was wondering who used to feed Sammy on the weekends when Mr. Maguire said, "Things have really changed since my day." He glanced around at the kids waiting at each door of the school. "We didn't stand in line waiting for the bell," he said. "We played on the playground before school."

"Why don't they let us do that anymore?" Connor asked. "I could use the time to perfect my back flip off the monkey bars."

"You just answered your own question, du-fus!" said Ryan.

But his dad shrugged. "There were no play-ground monitors back then either. It was the Wild West. Kids would fly off the swings, throw rocks, and get in fights."

"Sounds great!" said Ryan.

"We don't even *have* swings now," moaned Connor.

"Of course in those days," Mr. Maguire explained, "it didn't faze parents if their kid came home with a black eye or a bloody nose. I had a few in my day," he added modestly.

"Wow!" said Connor.

But Nate asked, "The teachers let kids fight?"

Mr. Maguire shrugged again. "There just weren't so many lame rules," he said, averting his eyes from the glare of Nate's glasses.

Just then, the main door opened, and the short, plump school secretary hustled out, followed by the tall, stooped figure of Ms Grieber, the Sherwood Elementary principal. Mrs. Katzen, the secretary, waved her arms and speed-walked toward a car that was illegally parked in the bus lane. Meanwhile, Ms Grieber surveyed the schoolyard.

Mr. Maguire turned his back, suddenly, and hunched his collar up around his ears.

"Ms Grieber's still here?" he asked in a low voice. "She must be old as the hills."

"She's retiring this year," Nate informed him.

As the car moved away, Ms Katzen hustled back to the office. Ms Grieber began strolling along the front of the building, her long legs covering a lot of pavement as she sauntered our way.

Mr. Maguire glanced quickly over his shoulder. "Uh, I've got to go boys," he said. "Have a good first day of school."

Like that's even possible, I thought, as the Dudes watched him hop on his motorcycle and speed away like a prisoner who'd been paroled.

Then (speaking of prison...) the bell rang. We all started to shuffle through the door, but Ms Grieber was suddenly beside us, barring the way with one long arm.

"Is that gum, Connor Maguire?" she asked sternly. "Not on the new carpets, mister," said the principal, holding out her hand.

I wondered if she was happy to be retiring from a job where she had to let kids spit their gum out in her palm.

Then, finally, we were in the building, smelling new carpet and sharpened pencils instead of the fresh air of freedom. The Dudes plodded down the fifth grade hall and split off into our separate classrooms like animals into cages.

A moment later, Ms Grieber's voice came over the intercom for morning announcements:

Good morning, Sherwood Seals!

Welcome back to our returning students. And a special welcome to our new kindergarteners.

Fifth-grade classes please report to the lunchroom now for a special assembly.

Yes! No teaching or learning. No work, not yet. The three fifth-grade classes spilled out into the hall, bunching and shoving, expanding to fill the space like wildebeests on the savanna.

"Single file, please!" cheeped Ms Finch, directing her class with the force of her cheerfulness.

Mr. Isaak used his superior height and threat of detention to goad his herd.

My teacher, Mrs. Hancock, ignored us entirely. Looking at her watch, she waded to the front of the mass of bodies.

"We're moving, people," she bellowed. Follow me!" Then she strode off without looking back.

Ryan shrugged and followed her. And I followed him. And, behind us, the rest of the fifth grade began moving with a great thundering of hooves—uh, tennis shoes.

In the lunchroom, Sammy the seal was painted around the walls in various roles: relaxing beneath a coconut tree on a desert island, swimming with a happy octopus, wielding paper and pencil underwater with a cheerful *school* of fish.

Seeing the paintings, I couldn't help an uneasy feeling in my stomach, as if the ghost of the real Sammy haunted this space. On the other hand, it could just be the smell.

At the far end of the cafeteria, several rows of folding chairs had been set up in front of the platform we called the stage. As our class reached the first row, Ryan stopped me in the aisle and turned to the kid behind me.

"After you," he said politely, motioning for Eddie Cramer to enter the row of seats first.

"After you," he said again for Kent Meadows and again for Sean Chang and then for a bunch of girls, until Ryan and I were the last two members of Mrs. Hancock's class to be seated about the middle of row three.

Next came Mr. Isaak's class with Deven leading. I had to give Mr. Isaak credit. It took most teachers at least an hour to discover that it's best to keep Deven up front where they can keep an eye on him.

Next to Deven was Nate. As soon as they were seated, Deven leaned across Nate to speak to the girl on Nate's other side.

"Hey, Teresa!" Yep. It was my neighbor, Teresa Gutierrez.

Teresa turned, narrowing her eyes at Deven. (I don't know why she would be suspicious. We had stopped talking in code in front of her. We even let her be a zombie in our hoard last summer!)

"Gina Bertrelli is trying to get your attention," Deven told her helpfully.

"Really?" said Teresa. She stood up and turned around to look over the fourth row toward Ms Finch's class at the back.

As she vacated her chair, Ryan, who'd been keeping an eye on the teachers, gave the signal for Operation Seat Swipe. In a flash, Connor stepped up on his empty chair in the last row then put his

foot on the seat back of the row in front of him, re-
lying on Jimmy Dutta's considerable weight to hold
the chair steady. From there, he did a quick two-
step on the seat backs of the next two rows and slid
into Teresa's chair like he'd always been there.

Teresa was still standing, making hand
signals to Gina Bertrelli, who was in the back row
(and probably confused by now). When the teachers began waving everybody down, Teresa nearly
sat on Connor's lap.

"What are you doing here?" said Teresa.
"Where's my chair?!" she added, as she looked
around to find the whole row filled.

Mr. Isaak noticed Teresa standing and directed her out of the row. "There are empty chairs
in the back," he said rubbing his beard wearily. I
heard him sigh as he approached Ms Finch and
said, "It's like this every year."

I guessed Ms Finch, as the new teacher, had
a lot to learn.

Anyway, Teresa ended up sitting next to
Gina, and the Dudes were together again, so it was
a win for everyone (except Gina, I guess).

Dude
Tycoons

"Long time no see!" said Deven.

The Dudes greeted each other with grins while the teachers shushed everybody.

Then Ms Larkey, the music teacher, flitted out onto the stage carrying a metal music stand. She adjusted it as tall as it would go, opened a laptop on it and clipped a microphone to the side. Then she pulled a remote control out of her pocket and pointed it at the blank wall in front of us.

Nothing happened.

Ms Larkey raised her reading glasses which dangled from a chain of rainbow crystals around her neck and squinted at the remote. Then she pushed another button. This time the screen descended with a motorized hum. Ms Larkey smiled, removed her glasses, and made a fluttery gesture to Ms Grieber.

The principal moved to center stage as Ms Larkey danced away. Ms Grieber looked out over the rows of fifth graders. Then she hunched her tall frame over the music stand to speak into the microphone.

"We have gathered here because I have a special announcement for the fifth graders," she said. "In the past, members of the fifth grade class have exhibited a certain...attitude," said Ms Grieber.

The Dudes nudged each other, and Ryan said, "She means Dad, I bet."

"As the senior class," Ms Grieber went on, "the fifth graders have a tremendous influence on the younger students in the school. Of course, we want the best behavior to be modeled. So we are going to provide you an incentive."

She clicked the laptop and this picture flashed on the pull-down screen behind her:

"This is a Coconut Buck," Ms Grieber announced, pointing to the screen. "It will be a special currency for fifth-graders only. You will be able to earn Coconut Bucks throughout the year for good behavior," she explained, "and trade them in for prizes at our end-of-the-year auction.

"This year-long program," she continued, "will not only establish good classroom habits but teach valuable economic principles...(blah, blah, blah)"

It was the same thing the teachers tried every year—paying the kids to follow rules like it was our job or something. We used to get popsicle parties until Nate's mom objected to rewarding kids with junk food. (Of course, it was the kids who *didn't* get junk food at home who had felt the most rewarded—namely Nate!)

Anyway, they changed it to an auction at the end of the year. The problem was, we'd long ago learned that there would be nothing at the auction that was as valuable as popsicles. It was mostly junk people's moms were trying to get rid of because their kids had bought it at last year's auction.

I was all set to start daydreaming through the rest of the assembly and maybe the rest of the year when Ms Grieber threw us a curve ball.

"As you may know, I came to Sherwood School thirty-five years ago as a teacher and eventually became principal," said Ms Grieber. "Since I am retiring in June," she went on, "the Fifth Grade auction will be stocked with items I've collected over all those years."

She chuckled a bit and added, "I'm finally going to clean out my closet!"

There was a rumble of noise from the crowd. Ms Grieber's closet was famous—or maybe I should say it was infamous. That's where she kept everything she confiscated from kids who got caught with things they shouldn't have at school.

The thing is, to get your stuff back, you had to bring your parents in. It was basically a ploy to embarrass the parents so Ms Grieber could be sure you got punished. But it had the effect of preventing most kids from ever trying to get their stuff back. After thirty-five years, Ms Grieber's closet was probably jam-packed.

"There might be anything in there—cell phones, fireworks, video games..." Connor said later that day when all the Dudes were together for recess.

We were gathered on the cargo net of the new playground. We call it the new playground because the Dudes sort of destroyed the old playground last summer (and helped the PTA raise money for a new one).

The new climber had a swinging bridge and a tunnel like the old climber. It also had a fire pole and a rock climbing wall, and the bright colors hadn't faded yet. The shredded rubber underneath was great for flicking at people too. But the best feature was a cargo net that stretched like a giant hammock from the climbing wall to the monkey bars and provided a valuable place to lie down during recess. We figured since the Dudes were sort of responsible for its existence, we had every right to use the cargo net as our headquarters.

"My little brother has a point," said Ryan.

(He knows Connor hates to be called 'little brother' just because he was born seven minutes later than Ryan.) "We know Ms Grieber's closet is full of stuff kids liked enough to carry around in the first place."

"Dude!" said Deven suddenly. "There could be a real Elephant Gun in there!"

By "real elephant gun" Deven meant a toy, of course. Years ago, the Foam Dart Company had built a toy called the Elephant Gun with a super-strong spring that could shoot darts over 200 feet! Then, somehow, they found out that, at close range, it could put out an eye, so the company stopped producing that model.

Of course, every kid alive wanted to get their hands on one of the few that were ever sold (and planned to be totally careful not to aim at anyone's eye)! Nate had found Elephant Guns on ebay going for hundreds of dollars. Some claimed there was one in Ms Grieber's closet, but no one had ever seen it.

I lay back on the net and stared into the sky. The Dudes could use a gun like that for long-range attacks on Teresa's treehouse and other important targets. In fact, we could probably carry on battles with other neighborhoods—assuming we could get the gun.

"That Elephant Gun rumor has been around for years," I pointed out. "How do we know it's true?"

Deven rocked the net with his exuberance. "My sister knows a guy who carpooled with the guy who says he lost it at school! And he's in high school now," he added.

"That would seem to put the tale in correct historical context," said Nate.

"If there *is* an Elephant in the auction, everyone will bid on it," Connor warned.

"But there are *five* of us!" I pointed out. "We can pool our money."

"Everybody start earning bucks now," ordered Ryan as he reclined against the ropes. "By the time of the auction, we'll be Coconut tycoons!"

 # *Dudes Democracy*

By the end of September, the Dudes had pretty much mastered school—at least the important classes: P.E., Recess, and Lunch.

And then there was music with Ms Larkey.

She was one of those adults who are so busy being artistic that they don't notice reality happening around them. Ms Larkey wore ruffled skirts and rainbow leotards. At music class, she danced around the room. And she sang her sentences like she was in an opera instead of in a portable building on the back side of the playground. On Tuesdays, when it was time to tromp across the soccer field to Ms Larkey's room, the fifth graders groaned.

On the other hand, the three fifth grade teachers breathed a sigh of relief. I know because Ryan and I actually heard them sighing as they gathered to chat in the hallway. At the mention of Coconut Bucks, we couldn't resist being late to music so we could hunch behind the laptop charging rack to listen:

"Our Coconut Buck economy seems to be booming," chirped Ms Finch cheerily.

"Classroom behavior has improved for the moment," agreed Mrs. Hancock.

"It's strange," said Mr. Isaac, rubbing his beard. "In my experience, fifth-graders usually find good behavior unprofitable."

Mrs. Hancock looked at him and nodded.

Ryan and I nodded too.

But Ms Finch said, "My students are very eager to please. Connor Maguire has practically taken over classroom cleanup!" She hesitated, then added reluctantly, "Of course, he's usually the *reason* the classroom needs cleaning."

Ryan and I nodded again.

"Still," Ms Finch went on, "I have to give him credit for enthusiasm."

"I don't know," said Mr. Isaac. "My years of teaching have made me suspicious of enthusiasm."

Unfortunately, the Dudes had to spend at least some of our time at school actually learning stuff that my dad swears he uses all the time in the "real world":

- math
- science
- language arts
- whatever social studies is

Nate called getting through the day "running the gauntlet", by which he meant "an ordeal involving attack from all sides." Ryan said it sounded like a great video game (more on that in chapter 12).

But when Mrs. Hancock announced that the whole fifth grade would be studying ancient Greece, I was actually interested.

See, the poet Homer is one of my heroes. He's the one who told the great epic stories of the Trojan War and the adventures of Odysseus. Homer preserved those awesome tales for the people of the future, just like I'm preserving the epic adventures of the Dudes by writing them down in the Chronicles. So Homer was sort of the Tyler Reynolds of the 8ᵗʰ century B.C.!

Having read Homer's stories, I knew that ancient Greece was chock full of gods and monsters and heroes and battles and exciting stuff like that. So, when Mrs. Hancock called out the page number, I eagerly opened my textbook and found...

Ancient Greek City-States: Cradle of Early Democracy

Yawn. Leave it to the teachers to find their way right to the boring part.

Turns out the Greeks are also known for giving us the exhilarating subject known as politics. Apparently, they used to run their cities by getting everybody together to debate ideas and vote on what to do—something that's called direct democracy.

The idea must have seemed wicked fresh back when people were used to having a king order them around. It probably took the average citizen

of Athens a while to get tired of listening to everybody's dumb ideas about the Feta Festival when all
he really wanted to do was get home and pick his
olives. Probably wasn't long before he was praying
for a Spartan attack just to liven things up!

Unfortunately, the fifth grade classes had to
experience this boredom for ourselves by holding
debates to choose our class colors.

In my class Mrs. Hancock limited the state-
ments to thirty seconds each because she didn't
want us to get off schedule. We had a quick vote,
and red and white won easily. Connor said Ms
Finch's class chose black and orange because Gina
Bertrelli said that was a classier combination than
red and blue. End of discussion. But, according
to Nate, things were a little more exciting in Mr.
Isaak's class.

To begin with, Teresa wanted purple and
gold because purple is her favorite color.

Nate took a quick survey of the fingernail
polish and hair clips in the room and determined
that purple was going to be popular among the
girls. On top of that, a lot of boys like purple and

gold because they just happen to be the colors of a nearby university with good sports teams. The rival university wears silver and blue, and that was the other choice. (Nate suspected that Mr. Isaak chose those color combos intentionally to cause trouble.)

It had sparked Nate's scientific interest in seeing if he could swing the vote the other way. But Nate was used to debating adults—you know, arguing that a word problem used incorrect grammar or pointing out that a unit title was inaccurate. I heard he had some pretty tough questions for God in Sunday School too. Teachers either love Nate or they hate him.

However, arguing with kids was different. Nate decided he needed someone who could speak their language.

That's when Deven stood up and started spouting verse, just like Homer:

> *"Ancient Greeks, my plea ain't fake.*
> *Please don't make this grape mistake!*
> *Purple and gold is sad and old!*

Silver and Blue is right for you!"

Okay. Not exactly like Homer, but it caught attention. Nate saw Deven's potential and tried to coach him.

"Associate our colors with something good," he whispered.

Deven told the class, "Blue and silver are the colors of Topflight foam darts! And the uniforms of the Space Police!" Then he put his fist over his heart in the Ninja salute. "Blue and silver reminds me of clear skies over Mount Sterling," he said.

Teresa, who was still standing at the front of the class, stared at him. "I don't even know what those things are," she said, like it was cool to be so ignorant.

According to Nate, that's when Deven departed a little from his coaching.

"She wants our class to have the colors of a bruise!" he said, raising his sleeve to show one he happened to have. "Do you want us to look like a flying people-eater?" Deven demanded. "Or Teresa's face?" he added desperately, pointing to Teresa, who, Nate had to admit, was turning a little purple.

"It was probably due to an excess of blood in the capillaries," Nate explained later, "indicating that she was about to explode."

Unfortunately, that's when Mr. Isaak stepped in to wearily advise that personal attacks were not allowed in class debates even though (as Nate helpfully pointed out) they *were* probably used in ancient Greek city-states.

Anyway, it was almost time for P.E., so each student got a pebble to put in the bowl for their choice of colors. That's how the Greeks voted—counting pebbles.

Purple and Gold won easily. But, even though his side lost, Deven had gotten a taste for politics.

That was just as well, because, the next week the teachers announced we were moving on from direct democracy to representative democracy. That's where the people elect leaders to decide things for them.

We would be electing a fifth grade council made up of six kids. And, to encourage competition, the teachers said those kids would each get a "salary" of two hundred Coconut Bucks a week.

Right away, nearly everybody in my class raised their hands for the free Bucks.

Then Mrs. Hancock explained the duties.

"This council will carry out certain jobs like making the morning announcements and planning student projects," she explained.

The hands of several loafers went down.

"They will also make an election speech," said Mrs. Hancock.

A few more hands went down.

"The student council will meet with Ms Grieber on a regular basis."

By this point, most kids had wised up and backed out. But guess who was still raising her hand...

"Teresa?!" said Ryan before school the next day.

He looked down the list that was posted on the door to the fifth grade hall. The other candidates were okay kids—not goofballs or anything. But they couldn't stand up to Teresa.

Teresa was crazy persuasive. Once she got her teeth into the council, who knows what she would decree: Bring Your Dog to Class Day? Painting the school purple? Renaming Sammy the Seal Samantha? I wasn't sure Ms Grieber herself could withstand Teresa's intimidation.

"Remember when Teresa dared us to build a treehouse in one day?" I reminded the Dudes. (In case you didn't know, that's how we ended up building a ninja training dojo in the crabapple trees in my backyard.)

"We've got to get someone on that council who won't be dancing to Teresa's ballet music," Ryan insisted.

Luckily, Deven was up for the challenge. "I'm throwing my hat in the ring!" he announced, grabbing the baseball cap off Connor's head and tossing it like a Frisbee.

It flew over the bike racks, across the bus

lane and bounced off Mr. Isaak's belly as he was crossing the parking lot with a travel mug in his hand.

Mr. Isaak looked our direction and sighed. Then he stepped over the cap and continued to chug coffee as he walked toward the entrance to school.

The Dude Candidate

The candidates had three days to come up with campaign promises and write their speeches. Nate helped Deven as much as he could.

On election day, the fifth graders were herded to another assembly. On the way, Ryan pulled me out of line to point to something carved on the side of the ancient water fountain. It was the letters KSM with a lightning bolt striking the K. It looked like this:

"Kevin Sean Maguire," said Ryan importantly. "That's my dad's logo!"

"Wow," I said. I figured neither of my parents was ever cool enough to have a logo.

As I leaned over to get a drink, I noticed two

kindergarteners standing there with a library pass. But, instead of going into the library, they were staring at me.

"Are you really a Dude?" one of them asked. I swallowed and nodded, but, before I could say anything else, Ryan pulled my arm.

"Come on," he said. "It's time for Operation Four to Tango."

Earlier in the day, Ryan had talked four kids in Mrs. Hancock's class into each saving seats for one of the others, which meant, by the time they figured out the mix-up, there were four open seats in the front row, perfect for Ryan, Connor, Nate, and me.

Deven would be onstage. He showed up wearing one of his dad's suit jackets over his T-shirt. His grandmother had pinned up the sleeves, and his mother had given him a little red handkerchief for his front pocket. (Deven's parents were kind of excited that their son was "beginning a career in public service." They saw this as the first step to the White House, I guess.)

"Look at me!" said Deven spreading his

arms with a glowing smile. "I'm a cand-i-dude!"

"Good luck," said Nate, giving Deven a shove up the stairs to the stage where there were chairs for the kids who were running.

Ms Larkey set up the music stand again.

Ms Grieber welcomed us all to the lunchroom (like we had any choice). Then she introduced each speaker.

The candidates from Mrs. Hancock's class went first, followed by the ones from Ms Finch's class. They mostly promised useless stuff like "upholding dignity" and "cherishing school spirit". The audience was shifting in their seats by the time we got to the four candidates from Mr. Isaak's class.

The first two kids did what everybody else had done. They slouched over the music stand, rattling the paper they were reading from and mumbling their promises. Then Teresa came to center stage.

She must have looked up "how to give a good speech" online. She stood straight and smiled out at the audience. She had her speech memorized. And she spoke clearly, looking proud but humble—which shows you right there what a tricky politician she was. From our place in the front row, the Dudes stared into Teresa's open mouth with dread.

She started off by proposing that an inspirational message be read over the intercom during morning announcements.

I saw Ms Grieber nod appreciatively at that, despite the retching noises the Dudes were making.

When the teachers had shushed the audience, Teresa continued. She also promised to get music played over the loudspeakers in the lunchroom while we were eating.

The Dudes winced, knowing she meant the music of Troy Diamond: a guy whose voice is even more piercing than the screams of the insane girls who worship him.

Finally, she vowed to introduce karate to the list of skills students learn in PE.

I frowned. Actually, that wasn't a bad idea.

The audience clapped hard after Teresa—probably because there was only one speech left.

Now it was Deven's turn.

"He doesn't have to beat Teresa," Nate reminded us. "To get on the council, he just has to appear more impressive than six out of the other ten candidates."

I crossed my fingers.

On his way to the music stand, Deven couldn't resist pretending to stumble across the stage.

Some kids tittered.

Having caught a laugh, Deven looked up and smiled his dazzling smile. I noticed there was no paper in his hand and was glad he'd memorized his speech so he would look more dignified.

Suddenly, Deven whipped the tiny scarf out of his pocket and let loose with a ridiculous, honking, sneeze! The audience jumped as his pocket square shot forcefully off the stage.

The rest of the audience guffawed while kids in the front row squealed and leaned to dodge the snot cloth.

Nate shook his head. "I wondered why he wanted my mini air pump," he whispered over the shushing of the teachers.

Finally, Deven went to the microphone.

I knew his promises were based on what Nate had told him was a successful Roman strategy for keeping the populace happy: bread and circuses—in other words: food and entertainment.

"As your student council representative," Deven announced, "I pledge to deliver the three P's."

He raised a finger with each promise.

"Popsicles on the playground! Popcorn for school assemblies! And pudding during standardized testing!"

The audience roared and stamped their feet.

The teachers hurried to quiet us down.

Mr. Isaak just shook his head.

"And that's not all!" said Deven like the guy selling cheese slicers on TV.

"I have lots of ideas for fun," Deven assured the crowd. "How about trampolines in the gym? War games on field day! Random Noise performing on Parents Night!"

The audience surged to their feet. I think

they would have swept Deven right off the stage except that Ms Grieber threatened detention if we didn't quiet down.

"This election is serious," Ms Grieber said, taking the stage. "Take a look at the candidates and vote for the ones who are responsible."

Behind her, I could see Teresa sitting straight and tall, with her hands folded and an earnest expression on her face. Deven looked like he was thinking about pudding.

"I urge you to choose leaders who are hard-working and reliable," said Ms Grieber. "You must elect those whose promises are believable, not pie-in-the-sky."

"Pie!" shouted Deven, raising a fourth finger.

Everything Ms Grieber had just said was designed to direct the voters away from Deven. And maybe it would have worked. But, like most people who enjoy making speeches, our principal didn't know when to quit. She just had to add one more thing:

"Remember this, students," she said. "Whomever you select will be helping to plan the fifth-grade field trip in the spring."

Behind Ms Grieber, Deven raised his eyebrows and smiled that dazzling smile again. There
was only one candidate who could promise what
the fifth-graders really wanted on our field trip.

Or maybe I should say, only one cand-i-
dude!

 # *Dudes of the Dead*

Gooooood morning, Sherwood Seals!

This is your fifth-grade Councilman, Deven Singh, here to give you the low down on what's up.

For your listening pleasure in the lunchroom today: the soothing sounds of Random Noise. Hooooot!

Now, if we could only do something about that random meat!

Here's today's inspirational message: Halloween is coming, so get your ghoul on! And remember: The Monster Mash is just the Funky Chicken with less Funk and more Mash.

Yep, that was Deven giving the inspirational message during the morning announcements. It turns out Teresa couldn't be there in the mornings because she's on the Safety Patrol. But Ms Grieber liked her idea so much that she asked for another volunteer.

Ms. Zito, the P.E. teacher liked Teresa's suggestion about teaching karate too, which was cool. Most of the kids like karate better than square dancing anyway. (Although Deven still do-si-dos occasionally.)

Speaking of scary stuff, Ryan had another spooky story from his dad. When school was out, he dragged us down to the end of the block where there was a stormwater collection pond.

"Dad says there used to be piranhas living here," he told us. "You couldn't see them, but, if you stuck your hand in the water..." he paused dramatically, "...it would be nothing but *bones* when you pulled it out!"

We all stared at the grassy banks sloping down to what was basically a big puddle.

"Piranhas are river fish," Nate pointed out. "This pond has no outlet."

"That's why they never escaped," Ryan insisted.

"People keep piranhas as pets," Connor explained. "Dad said somebody probably got tired of buying hamburger to feed them and dumped them here."

Ryan nodded.

"That's why the city fenced it in and put up these danger signs," he added, pointing to a sign that showed a stick man amid some stylized waves and a red slash across the whole thing.

"They probably didn't want kids to swim here," said Nate reasonably.

"Yeah, because they'd get eaten!" Connor put in.

Ryan continued the story. "Luckily, Sherwood had a drought that summer, and the pond dried up. But guess what they found at the bottom?"

"Bones of small animals!" Connor finished, earning a shove from Ryan.

"Oooh, spooky!" said Deven as we all stared through the fence—well, all but Ryan and Connor, who were too busy trying to push each other's faces through the chain link.

After that, we went over to Deven's house.

Deven's grandmother had recently been to a farmers' market, I guess. She served roasted pumpkin seeds and fresh apple cider on the Singhs' front porch, which was now decorated with a tasteful assortment of pumpkins and corn stalks and Dudes.

Deven was using a friendly scarecrow to demonstrate the finer points of the monster mash when a car loaded with teenagers pulled up to the curb.

Deven's sister, Shaila got out and stomped across the lawn in designer boots.

"Don't dance with the decorations where my friends can see," she ordered her brother. Then she clumped up the steps and across the porch without a glance at the rest of us.

"So lame!" she muttered before the door slammed.

"Your sister is rather formidable," Nate commented.

"Tell me about it!" agreed Deven. "She's the meanest contender in the whole history of debate team. Coming after her, it's hard to impress my parents no matter how serious I am—isn't that right, Snootie?" Deven said, turning to speak to a gourd that looked like it had a big, warty nose.

The gourd nodded.

Ryan sat down on a straw bale. "Forget Shaila, Dudes," he said. "We need ideas for Halloween—something cool."

"We could be ninjas," suggested Nate.

It was true. We had been ninjas all summer. We had created a secret code and built a dojo for training. One night we had even dressed in black and glided silently all over the neighborhood. It had been great—with only three or four minor mishaps.

"Not ninjas," Ryan decided. "Prowling secretly through the night is one thing. But a bunch of ninjas clomping around ringing doorbells with sacks in their hands is lame."

Ryan and Connor's dad was always talking about things being lame, and now Ryan was doing it too. In fact, I had noticed that the tendency to point out lameness was a common characteristic of cool people. It's like a public service, I guess.

"We could be something else," I said. "You know, a group costume. Like a horse or something."

"Who'd be the head?" asked Deven.

"And who'd be the tail?" asked Connor.

"Five guys won't fit in a horse costume," Nate pointed out.

"We could be one of those big dragons like they have in Chinese parades," I said.

"Who'd be the head?" asked Deven.

"And who'd be the tail?" asked Connor.

"And how do we hold the candy bag?" asked Deven. He picked up my backpack with his teeth and growled.

I made a mental note to wipe my backpack strap later.

"Group costumes are no good for trick or treat," argued Connor. "Think about it, guys. One costume. One bag. One-fifth the candy."

"Who wants to go trick-or-treating anyway?" said Ryan.

We all stared at him.

"The cool thing about Halloween isn't candy," he announced.

"It isn't?" said Connor.

"It's scaring people. Listen!"

Ryan had the look he always has when he's about to come out with a great idea, so we listened.

"I bet we could scare people real good with a haunted house," said Ryan. "Like in the horror movies Dad watches."

"What people?" asked Deven.

Ryan shrugged.

"People from the neighborhood, like Teresa and everybody," he explained. "We've just gotta think of ways to make the house scary."

"Mom says our house is already scary," said Connor.

She wasn't the only one.

"A haunted house? Like in the horror movies?" my Mom asked when I told her Ryan's idea. She shuddered like she was picturing Connor in the dining room with a hockey mask and a chainsaw.

I tried to explain that our approach was more spooky than gory, but I didn't have much luck, and neither did the other guys. None of the parents were willing to have a bunch of kids traipsing through their living rooms on Halloween night.

Luckily, this didn't slow Ryan down.

"We'll do it outside," he said.

"A haunted yard?" asked Deven.

"A haunted *grave*yard," said Ryan.

And that's how it started. We decided to set it up in my side yard because our hedge would hide everything from the sidewalk. Also, my dad said he knew there were no utility lines there, which is important when you're digging a hole. (I'll explain the hole later.)

We started making gravestones by painting old boxes with funny names like: Ben Shott, Frank N. Stein, and Ima Corpse. Then we got some stuff to spook the place up.

Deven recorded his best howls and evil laughs on his phone. And I borrowed a cauldron from my neighbor. Actually, it was sort of a black metal bucket that Mrs. Kostenko grows petunias in in the summer, but she was nice about lending it. Mom even let us use old sheets to hang in the trees as ghosts. It was all coming together.

"Man, we could charge money for this," said Deven.

"Too bad nobody carries Coconut Bucks when they're trick-or-treating," Nate pointed out.

"Even better," said Connor. "We'll charge candy. It'll make up for not trick-or-treating. Trust Connor to have his eye on the candy quotient.

"Okay, everybody come up with a scary costume," Ryan commanded.

"I call skeleton!" said Connor. He already had a t-shirt with glow-in-the-dark bones.

"I'm gonna be a mummy," said Ryan. "Mom's got tons of bandages." (I figured Ryan and Connor's mom being a nurse wasn't the only reason they kept a lot of first aid supplies, but I didn't say anything.)

"I already have what I need for my ghost costume," said Nate thoughtfully.

"This is gonna be awesome!" said Ryan. Of course, he always says that.

On Halloween the guys came over right after supper.

"Dudes! Guess who I am!" Deven shouted.

He was hanging upside down from our maple tree at the time.

"An opossum?" Nate guessed.

"I'm a bat!" said Deven, swinging himself down and swaying dizzily across the lawn.

"Bats can fly," Nate pointed out.

"And see in the dark," said Connor, as Deven crashed into him.

"I'm a vampire bat!" said Deven spreading his cape like wings and laughing ghoulishly to show his fangs. "Mwah-ha-ha-ha!"

Nate had pulled a bag of flour out of this canvas backpack he was wearing.

"Who are you supposed to be?" I asked him.

"Private Harrison Pierce," he replied.

We all stared at his blue uniform.

"Who's that?" Ryan asked. He was sitting in the grass wrapping bandages around his legs.

"He was a soldier who died at the second battle of Fort Wagner on July 18th, 1863," Nate answered. "My father is a Civil War buff," he added. "He helped me with the costume."

Deven was confused as usual. "I thought

you were gonna be a ghost," he said.

"Dude, a guy who died in 1863 would *have* to be a ghost!" Ryan pointed out.

Then Deven took the baggie of flour and helpfully blew handfuls at Nate until he looked like either a ghost or a military pastry chef.

I had decided to be a zombie like in Zombie Bash II. When the Dudes made our zombie movie last summer, I had played one of the zombie *hunters*. But being undead looked like fun. Halloween was my chance to try it out.

The costume was easy enough—my oldest clothes, some gray face paint and fake blood. I used Mom's hair gel too—to plaster my hair into a wild mess. It looked even better after I was all dirty from digging.

Oh yeah. See I'd thought of how I could dig my way out of the grave just like the zombies do in the cut scene from Zombie Bash II. (That's where the big hole comes in.)

I just had to lie in the hole with a brown blanket over me. Then the guys would shovel a light layer of potting soil on top to make it look good. When someone came along, I'd moan a little and claw my way out. I figured it would be the biggest surprise of the whole haunted graveyard.

We got it all set up before dark and decided to try it out on Jayden.

My little brother was sitting on the front steps, dressed up in his superhero costume with a jacket on over it because of the cold. I could tell he was nervous about leaving the house. He's never gotten over his fear of the man-in-the-moon. (Have you ever really looked at that guy?)

Ryan brought Jayden to the graveyard.

When I heard their voices, I figured they were close enough and started clawing my way out of the hole. I really hammed it up too, moaning and growling and stumbling around like my limbs weren't attached right.

But Jayden just frowned. "Your clothes are really dirty, Tyler," he commented.

Ryan cracked up.

Well, what did I expect? Jayden's never played Zombie Bash II. Mom says it's too scary for him, but maybe it's just too messy.

Right then Connor popped up from behind a gravestone wearing his skull mask. "Trick or treat!" he said.

Jayden took one look and screamed. (Oh yeah, he has a thing about masks too.) He turned around and ran for the front steps.

Ryan tried to stop him but tripped over his bandages.

Then Mom came rushing out with little Leon in his pumpkin suit balanced on her hip. I guess Jayden running with Ryan tottering after him and the rest of us laughing gave her the wrong idea. She beckoned us over with one of those mom looks.

"Tyler, I don't want you boys finding fun by scaring your little brother," she said.

"We weren't trying to scare him, Mom—I mean, not him more than anybody else," I tried to explain. "It *is* a haunted graveyard."

"You know masks bother Jayden," she said.

"But *he* wears a mask half the time."

"Weaknesses don't always make sense," said Mom.

She turned to Ryan. "What if it was spiders?" (I guess Dad had told her about the camping trip last summer when Ryan refused to use the outhouse because of spiders.)

Ryan tried to shrug, but it was really more of a shudder. And his bandages fell over his face again so that it was kind of muffled when he spoke.

"Don't worry, Mrs. Reynolds," he said. "Jayden was just helping us test our product. Now we know the terror is for big kids only."

"I want to go again!" said Jayden immediately, so I guess he wasn't *too* traumatized.

Mom eyed us all suspiciously.

Speaking of eyes, the way my baby brother, Leon, was staring at my messy hair with baby pumpkin eyes, he was kinda freaking *me* out.

"Come on, Mom," I whined. "It'll be dark soon."

That jolted her into action. "Right," she said. She grabbed Jayden's hand and dragged him off to trick-or-treat, his cape flying out behind.

As soon as Mom was gone, the dudes and I ran around setting up the sound effects and dry ice, which, when we dropped it in the cauldron of warm water, made fog that curled like ghostly fingers over the lawn.

Nate and Connor found their hiding places, and Deven climbed back into the tree. Last thing, I climbed into my "grave" and lay down. I pulled the blanket up over my face and felt the pitter-patter as Ryan sprinkled dirt over me.

Being undead gives you a different perspective on a lot of things. Lying in the grave, I could hear sounds all over the neighborhood: a dog barking, doorbells ringing, kids laughing and calling "trick-or-treat", and, of course, Deven's werewolf howls from where he'd hung a speaker in the tree.

I wondered how long I'd have to wait for a customer. I had an itch on my back—just an itch, not something crawling in the dirt underneath me. I wished Mom had never said anything about spiders, though. It's not that I was afraid of them like Ryan. I don't mind meeting a spider in the light of day, above ground.

Don't think about it, I told myself, because now I could hear voices much closer. One of them was definitely Teresa. (Her voice tends to carry.) Only I couldn't stand the itch anymore and shifted my shoulder-blades a little to scratch it. But that made some of the potting soil fall off the blanket and down into my hair.

Meanwhile, I could definitely hear giggling. Perfect. A whole gang of girls. Boy, would they be scared!

Was it just dirt that seemed to be moving on my scalp?

Ryan was telling them to hand over some candy.

Teresa was arguing. She didn't want to give up her full-size Hershey bar.

I heard an eerie whisper from a nearby skeleton: "Whoa! Who's giving out *those*?"

A tickle was now moving up my neck to my ear. I tried to ignore it, but, when I felt eight hairy legs, I panicked.

"Aaaggh!" I screamed, throwing off the sleeping bag and sending a shower of dirt onto Ryan and the girls.

By now I was pretty sure there were at least

twenty of them—spiders, not girls, though that would be scary too. I leaped out of the hole and started dancing around in the yard, scraping myself all over. I was the fastest-moving zombie you ever saw!

It's not like I was paying attention at the time, but it turns out Teresa was wearing a blue checked dress and red shoes like Dorothy from The Wizard of Oz, and of course, she had a little basket on her arm to hold Toto. Only Toto wasn't in the basket.

Suddenly I felt a sharp pain on my ankle.

"Teacup!" Teresa yelled at the same time I yelled, "Help!"

Connor and Nate popped out from behind their gravestones, and Deven fell out of the tree.

At this show of force, Teresa's little dog yelped and took off like a black and tan streak.

"Teacup!" screamed Teresa again, dropping the basket.

"I'll catch him!" vowed Ryan, but he took about three steps before his bandages fell over his eyes and he crashed into one of our hanging ghosts.

He yelled for Connor and Nate to pick him up.

Meanwhile, the girls were laughing and screaming and chasing after Teacup, who zigzagged through the yard before taking off down the sidewalk.

Regaining his feet, Ryan ran after the girls, his bandages flapping.

Connor, Nate, and Deven followed Ryan as always.

And, once I had checked for blood on my sock, I took off after the others, abandoning the gravestones, the basket, and the cauldron with dry ice still bubbling.

 # *Dudes Unplugged*

Where does a little dog go when being chased by a mummy, a vampire, a ghost, a skeleton, a zombie and a bunch of screaming girls?

Home.

We chased him out of the cul-de-sac, around the corner, down Sherwood Lane, and straight to Teresa's front porch where he disappeared through his little dog door.

Teresa turned around and started to yell at us for scaring her dog. But that's when the front door opened and her mother looked out.

We all stood there like, well, zombies. Mrs. Gutierrez is the middle school principal. And a principal is a scary sight on Halloween or, really, anytime.

"Well?" said Mrs. Gutierrez examining us like we were about to T-P her yard. "Aren't you supposed to say 'trick-or-treat'?" she asked.

So, of course, we did. It turned out Teresa's mom was the one giving out full-size Hershey bars. "If you're going to do something, do it right," is what Mrs. Gutierrez said.

The Dudes didn't argue. In fact, we decided to go on from there to the other houses on Teresa's block. Trick-or-treating was a lot less danger- ous than running a haunted graveyard—and you couldn't argue with the rewards.

When we got back with all the candy we could carry in Nate's ammo satchel, we found Tere- sa's basket in the yard. Of course, the Dudes were too honest to keep the loot for ourselves. Besides which, it was mostly these little boxes instead of candy.

The dudes had gotten some of those too. Each box had a colorful round or oval piece of rub- ber.

"They're not edible!" Connor reported, spit- ting one out into my zombie hole. "What kind of Halloween treat is that?"

"They're Sushirasers," Teresa told us when

we returned her basket. "Oh my gosh! Did you take any?" she asked, snatching her basket out of Ryan's hand.

"Of course not," he answered, offended. "Why do you care so much?"

Teresa wrapped her arms around the basket the way she usually wrapped them around Teacup. "Never mind," she told him, shutting the door.

"Dudes!" said Ryan. "We gotta find out about Sushirasers."

"According to the internet they are popular collectibles," Nate told us the next day. "My research shows that a complete set of twenty-five— enough to fill the large-size Bento Box—is worth nearly five hundred dollars on the open market."

It was a rare sunny day, and we were catching some rays on the three platforms of our tree-house dojo.

"We got like fifteen of those little boxes on Halloween!" said Connor, stepping off the middle platform and catching a tree limb to swing himself down to the lower level. (He could perform this kind of maneuver because we had wisely designed our treehouse without walls.)

"But, according to my research, there are two sushis that are very rare," said Nate, "Dragon King and Dancing Shrimp."

Sure enough, once we'd opened all our boxes, we had seven Tekka-Maki's, three Kappa-Maki's, a Monkey Face, a California Roll, a Butterfly, and two Sashimi's.

"Dang!" said Connor, looking at the bento chart Nate had printed for us. "We need both the rare ones plus seventeen more kinds."

"We're not trying to get a complete set anyway," I pointed out. "That's a girl thing."

"I'd *sell* it to a girl for five hundred dollars," said Connor. He opened the fridge and perused the supply of Halloween candy.

Yeah, the dojo had a fridge—a small one. Now that the weather was getting colder, we didn't need to plug it in, but, being air-tight, it still made a good place to stash snacks. We used to have the fridge and a whole lot more plugged in to the electrical outlet in the shed. But now that Dad had decided to use the shed for his home office, everyone was pitching in to help:

- Mom had bought a second-hand collapsible baby cage for when Leon had to "help" Dad in his office.
- Jayden had painted a bunch of pictures for the office walls.
- Granddad had made frames to use on the shed windows for screens next summer "so it won't become a sweat box," he said.
- And the Dudes had gone unplugged.

Today, for instance, we were using Nate's speakers on *battery* power to blast our favorite group: Random Noise. Just then we heard the intro to "Rock Down the Walls" and chimed in on the "Hooooot!" which is a battle cry that marks the beginning of the song.

Dad came out of the shed with a hammer in his hand from putting up shelves.

"Guys, can you hold down the noise?" he called.

"That's *Random* Noise, Mr. Reynolds," supplied Ryan helpfully.

Dad made a face. "It sounds like a sick owl."

"That's just the singing," Deven explained, putting on his Random Noise hair and shaking it.

Dad shook his head too and went back inside.

Deven had paid for that Random Noise wig with his allowance. When his father saw it, Mr. Singh had nearly torn out his own hair while muttering about the waste of perfectly good money.

In case you don't know, the guys from Random Noise have long hair which is styled kind of... well, randomly. I guess it's a theme, because hunks of it are also colored randomly in red, green, yellow, purple, and blue. I had seen more than a few kids wearing colors in their hair when we were trick-or-treating last night. Which reminded me:

"Hey guys, come on," I said. "Dad says we have to fill up the hole from the haunted graveyard before somebody falls in it or something."

The Dudes climbed down out of the treehouse dojo—all except for Connor, who had to make a grand exit, sailing down the zipline to Flying Kick the shed.

As the *boom!* reverberated, Dad came staggering out with his eyes goggling to watch us walk around to the side yard.

We only had one shovel. While we took turns un-digging the hole, Nate made his report on the Elephant Gun:

"Based on my internet research, I can predict that a working Elephant Gun on the open market would cost upwards of four hundred dollars," said Nate.

"I have also determined the theoretical exchange rate between ordinary dollars and Coconut Bucks," he explained. "Of course, the Sherwood School economy is a closed system, and therefore..."

"Just cut to the chase," Ryan interrupted. "What'll the gun cost us at the fifth-grade auction?"

"My estimate is that the bidding may go as high as 45,000 Coconut Bucks," Nate replied.

Wow! That sounded like a lot.

"Divided five ways, it's only nine thousand a

piece," said Connor hopefully.

"Right! We can save that much," said Ryan.
"It's already been two months. How much do we
have?"

"Around seven hundred Bucks," Nate answered.

"A piece?" I asked.

Nate shook his head. "Total," he said.

Not exactly a fortune. The problem was that
teachers mostly gave out Bucks for good behavior
like paying attention in class, being quiet during
reading time, and turning in your homework. Nate
and I weren't doing too badly there, but the rest of
the Dudes weren't big earners.

Ryan usually zoned out whenever a teacher
was speaking. (He claimed it sharpened his mental
focus—sort of like meditating, I guess.) Connor's
homework tended to get destroyed in bizarre acci-
dents. And Deven...well, he wasn't going to get rich
on quiet behavior.

Luckily, Deven had his student council salary. And Nate got paid for helping reboot crashed
laptops in tech class.

The problem was you could *lose* Bucks too. Ryan and I had both lost some for talking. (Mrs. Hancock was kind of old fashioned about kids who multi-task while she teaches.) Connor had lost some for water fountain stunts (don't ask). And then there was Deven, who lost Bucks for things like reading his book report in a Beyoncé voice.

Nate continually lost Bucks by forgetting to turn in his library books or to put his name on his homework or by losing his pencils or his jacket or his science project. (Nate's kind of absent-minded. That's probably because he's always using his brain for thinking instead of anything practical.)

The teachers kept track of all the pluses and minuses and paid you at the end of the week—if there was anything left.

"It's a slow economy," I complained, throwing down the shovel.

"Not for girls," said Connor. "I heard Gina bragging she had nearly two thousand Bucks already. And Teresa does Bulletin Board Buddies and Library Helper and..."

"Relax," said Ryan. "The girls won't be bidding against us for the Elephant Gun."

It was Nate who pointed out the real danger: "Suppose some of the *boys* have better earning potential than we do," he said. "If they should decide to band together..."

"Nate's right," I said. "It's a big risk."

Ryan shook his head. "What we need is to get some of those Bucks out of the girls' hands."

I didn't know how we could do that, but, as usual, Ryan had an idea.

Dudes "R" Us

Good morning, Sherwood Seals.

Today the school nurse has this announcement:
The flu is going around. Please wash your
hands BEFORE and AFTER touching anything.

Ms Grieber has this announcement: Random
Noise has been banned from the lunchroom, and
hooting has been banned from the morning announcements. Awww!

Today's lunchroom music is: "Don't Brush Me
Off" by Troy Diamond. Good luck keeping your
lunch down.

Today's inspirational message is: Sharing is
caring—except with the flu...or Troy Diamond.

As soon as the announcements were over,
the Dudes got busy with Ryan's plan, which was,
basically, to sell our Sushirasers to the girls. Since
we'd already opened all the boxes we had, we could
offer the girls the chance to purchase the exact Sushis they needed with Coconut Bucks rather than

taking a chance on the wrapped Sushis they had to buy with real money. Nate called that a "value add".

We had sixteen to sell at 300 Bucks a pop. (We had even dug up my zombie hole again to get the one that Connor tried to eat—half price because of the tooth marks.)

The Sushis sold like, well, like fancy raw fish, I guess. Of course, Teresa didn't buy any. She said the "right" way was to buy a box and be surprised. But lots of other girls were happy to get our Sushis and to spend classroom currency. By the end of the day, we had 4800 extra Bucks to add to our total.

After school, I walked over to Nate's house to watch him put the Bucks in his vault. (Nate had rigged his closet with an alarm that signals his computer if it's been triggered. Of course, he could no longer keep *clothes* in his closet because his mom kept triggering the alarm trying to put away laundry.)

Anyway, I leaned against a towering stack of folded shirts in Nate's room while Nate entered the total in his spread sheet and stashed the cash. When we were done congratulating ourselves, I headed home.

Good Morning Sherwood Students.

Murray Downes said he saw snow flurries this morning. Let's all cross our fingers it wasn't just powdered sugar on his glasses. A snow day would come in handy before the math test!

Music in the lunchroom will be "Let It Snow" sung by Troy Diamond, who sounds like the cold already gave him a sore throat.

Now, for Today's Inspirational Message: Remember, friends, even in the darkest hour of social studies, someone somewhere is having pudding.

It's probably just as well that none of the adults ever pay attention to the morning announcements. Deven says, in the office, the secretary, Mrs. Katzen, is too busy signing in kids who are late and calling the parents of kids who made it to school on time but have already decided they are sick and want to go home.

Meanwhile, in homeroom, the teachers are

too busy checking roll and reprimanding the kids who are coming in with a late note from the office.

None of the Dudes managed to go home sick and the promised snow never came, so we spent a dismal week actually going to class and learning stuff. And, in the meantime, we earned as many Coconut Bucks as we could—which wasn't many.

We held a meeting at my house to discuss tactics for getting more Bucks.

"Too bad we're sold out of Sushirasers," said Connor.

"The market is still strong," Nate predicted. "We could sell more if we had them."

"You're telling me," said Connor. "Gina wants her full Bento!"

"This Sushiraser thing is a Coconut gold mine," Ryan said. "The girls will pay 300 Coconut Bucks for one of those little packets. And my mom can buy a crate of them for us at the warehouse store!"

Mrs. Maguire buys everything at the warehouse store, where you can pile your cart high with whole cases of stuff. She says she doesn't like to take a chance on running out of food with Connor in the house.

"The warehouse store costs *real* money," I pointed out, flopping down in the recliner.

We had the house to ourselves. Mom was back at work this week, and Dad had taken Jayden and Leon with him to buy groceries.

So far, not much had changed, having Dad at home. He was looser than Mom on screen time, but he expected me to do more chores, so it pretty much evened out. (Really, if I wasn't so careful with my time, you wouldn't be reading these epic adventures today.)

Ryan perched on the back of the couch, resting his feet on a pile of laundry I was probably supposed to be folding.

"We have a plan to use Sushirasers to get Coconut Bucks," he said confidently. "Now we just need a plan to get real money to buy Sushirasers."

"Wouldn't it be simpler to save our real money to buy something we want in the first place?" Nate asked. He was sitting cross-legged on the floor like the picture on the front of his <u>Medita-</u>

tion for Ninjas book.

Deven was on the floor too. But he was making faces at the happy crocodile on the front of Leon's diaper bag, which was on the coffee table. (I hoped Dad wouldn't need a diaper while he was out—for Leon, I mean.)

Connor was sprawled on the couch tossing a pillow into the air with his hands and catching it with his feet.

The pillow sailed past Ryan's face. "We won't find an *Elephant Gun* at the warehouse store," he reminded us.

There was silence as everyone thought what it would feel like to get their hands on a legend. But Nate had doubts. (He also had some money he was saving to buy a programmable robot.)

"What if we spend our real money on Sushirasers to get fake money for the auction and the Elephant Gun doesn't exist?" he asked. "All those Coconut Bucks would be worthless."

"Nate's right," said Connor, sitting up. "We need proof that Ms Grieber has one in her closet."

"If we could just get into her office," said

Ryan. As usual, when he was thinking, he enhanced his concentration by flicking Connor in the back of the head.

"A programmable robot would be very useful for such a mission," Nate mused.

"Hey! I'm on the student council!" said Deven, like he was just remembering. "I could go talk to the principal any time, if I had an idea for something council-y."

We all waited...

...but he didn't think of anything.

"It's not as easy as walking into her office," Nate warned.

"Yeah," Connor put in, jumping to his feet and out of range of Ryan's flicking finger. "Just yesterday, Gina Bertrelli had to turn over her smartphone," he informed us. "I heard her telling a bunch of girls that Ms Grieber keeps her closet locked so valuable stuff like that doesn't go missing."

I could believe that—I mean about the bunch of girls. There was always a group of girls around Gina Bertrelli. I guess it's because Gina had the knack of making everything that happened to her sound impressive.

If a dog peed on her lawn it was because she had the best rose bushes.

If she got lost on the way to the mall, it was the epic adventure of a lifetime.

If she got sparkle marker on her dress, it was a loss to the world of fashion—and every girl in school went out and bought sparkle markers, of course. (Come to think of it, I bet *she* started the Sushiraser craze!)

Meanwhile, Ryan was still working on his plan. "It's better if we go in when Ms Grieber's not there," Ryan was saying. "And we'll need a key to the closet," he added, like it was nothing.

"Oh yeah!" said Deven. "We could just lift the keys from her blazer pocket." He reached his hand into the diaper bag and came out with Snappy Frog attached to his fingers.

"Ahhh!" he yelled in mock pain, rolling around on the floor.

Meanwhile, Connor tried pickpocketing Ryan's hoodie and ended up in a half-nelson.

"Who else has a key?" Nate asked over the noise.

"Mr. Wilkins, the janitor?" I suggested.

Nate shook his head. "He keeps his keys on a chain attached to his pants."

Deven stopped fighting the frog and leaped to his feet. "I can see it now," he said. "Man, what happened to my keys? Forget the keys, what happened to your pants?!"

As Deven mimed comical naked embarrassment, Ryan had a breakthrough.

"The school secretary must have keys to everything in the office," he said.

"Mrs. Katzen?" I asked, feeling my eyebrows climb up my forehead. "She's scarier than Mr. Wilkins and Ms Grieber put together," I said. "We'll never pickpocket her."

"She doesn't keep her keys in her pocket," said Connor from under Ryan's arm.

Ryan released him so he could explain.

"See, one time I had this nosebleed," Connor began. (A lot of his stories involve injuries.)

"Silvia Drinkwater was already there with

a bee sting so she got the cot in the nurse's room," he went on, "and I was lying on the floor. Anyway, the nurse needed to check if Silvia was allergic, so Mrs. Katzen unlocked the student records for her. When she was done, I saw her hang the keys on the back of the metal file cabinet. They must have a magnetic key chain," Connor concluded.

"Not bad, little brother!" said Ryan, slapping him overly hard on the back. "We can get the keys. Now we just need to pick a time when Mrs. Katzen is away from her desk..."

"Lunchtime," said Nate. (You know Nate *never* gets sent to the office, but his mom is there practically every day doing volunteer work, and I guess she observes things.)

"Mrs. Katzen is on a diet," Nate explained. "According to my mom, she eats in the staff lounge every day where she can heat her frozen meal in the microwave and read a fitness magazine. She should be away from her desk for a good half-hour."

"Perfect!" said Ryan. "We'll pull our caper then. We'll take the keys for long enough to open the closet and snoop around. Then we'll return them before Mrs. Katzen even finishes lunch.

"Piece of cake!" he said, snapping his fingers.

"Aren't you forgetting something?" I pointed out. "We have to get Ms Grieber out of her office too."

Ryan smiled the way he does when a plan comes together. "For that, we need a student council-y idea," he said.

Dudes Impossible

Good morning, Sherwood Seals.

The first annual Lunch Buddies Luncheon be-
gins today.

Welcome parents. We hope you'll never forget
this eating experience.

But, if you do, we'll see you next year.

Today's lunch will be accompanied by the
sweet tones of Ms Grieber making her speech
to the parents about the Buddy-fication of
Lunch. Hum along, if you can.

Inspirational message of the day: If you can't
stand the meat, stay out of the kitchen.

    I don't know how Deven convinced Teresa
and the rest of the student council to run with Ryan's Lunch Buddies idea. (It might have involved
shadow puppets.)

    Luckily, Ms Grieber took the bait.

    Anyway, Lunch Buddy Day was a big success—maybe too big. Surprisingly, a lot of parents were willing to show up in the middle of the day and eat lunchroom food to show support for their kids. (I'm not sure whether to feel good about that, actually.)

Nate's mom was there, of course. Deven's grandmother showed up too. Even Mr. Maguire came.

My dad was there, carrying Leon in a pouch on his chest. "This is what I quit my job for," he told me, which I thought was kinda sad.

Then he added, "You're just lucky I don't have any clients yet. As soon as I get some clients, I'll be too busy for things like this."

I just smiled and nodded about Dad's imaginary clients as we walked into the lunchroom. Unfortunately, that's where "piece of cake" became "mission impossible" because the Dudes hadn't figured on having to pull off the whole caper under the very noses of our parents.

One thing was going well, though. As Ryan predicted, Ms Grieber couldn't resist making a speech to the guests. As she took her place beneath the Lunch Buddy Day banner (which was colored with sparkle markers, of course), the Dudes made eye contact across the crowded lunchroom tables. Project Pachyderm was a go.

Our first challenge would be to make a clean getaway from our lunchroom buddies. That was no problem for Nate who simply introduced his mother to Deven's grandmother. Mrs. Howe right away started talking about volunteer opportunities at the school, and Nani was trapped by her sense of courtesy. Neither woman noticed when Deven and Nate slipped away from Mr. Isaak's table, leaving their trays of pizza and tater tots behind.

Strangely, Mr. Maguire headed off to the bathroom as soon as Ms Grieber made her appearance. That left Ryan and Connor free to station themselves at the door and be ready to run interference if Ms Grieber should decide to leave the lunchroom.

At Mrs. Hancock's table, my dad was already pretty distracted by Leon and Jayden, but I didn't take chances.

"I'm gonna get more pudding, Dad," I told

him.

He nodded vaguely as I left the table. But, just for insurance, on my way out the door, I mentioned to Teresa and her friends that my baby brother was visiting. Just as I had hoped, the girls swarmed all over him in a second, cooing and giggling and completely blocking Dad's view of the exit.

Out in the hall, Deven took up his position as lookout in case any of the parents should decide to visit the office (people who will voluntarily eat in the lunchroom might do anything).

Through the glass office door, Nate and I could see Mrs. Katzen glance at the clock then get up from her desk, right on time.

The three of us Dudes studied the plush seal in the trophy case as she passed so as not to arouse suspicion. When the secretary was safely in the staff lounge, though, we doubled back, and Nate and I crept into the outer office.

The door to Ms Grieber's office was closed. I reached behind the filing cabinet. Sure enough, there were the keys. My heart pounding, I unlocked the door, and we tip-toed into the principal's office.

There it was—the closet. I put the key in the lock and twisted the knob.

Nate had studied online pictures of the Elephant Gun so as to quickly identify it. But, as the door swung open, we couldn't see much. There were deep shelves on all three sides of the closet, running floor to ceiling. And the shelves were crowded with junk: toys, weapons, tech...stuff going back thirty years, I guess. There were no labels. It was dusty. And the stuff on the front of the shelves hid the stuff at the back.

"We need a light," said Nate, stepping into the closet and waving his hands overhead for a string to pull.

It was about that time that I heard a terrible noise. It sounded like a saber-toothed lion being sucked into the La Brea Tar Pits. The noise was deadened by the glass door that stood between us, but, clearly, Deven was trying to get my attention.

When we were prepping for the mission, Deven had practiced a warning signal for Ms Grieber's approach. It was the call of the pied-billed grebe. He'd looked it up himself for authenticity ("I'm not just a pretty face, you know," Deven had told us.)

But the sound he was making now was more like a...CAT! I slunk to the outer office and peeked out the door. Sure enough, Mrs. Katzen was returning from the staff lounge with a steaming tray in her hand. She must have decided to eat at her desk today!

With only seconds to spare, I raced back and shut the closet door with Nate inside. Then I stepped back into the outer office, pulling Ms Grieber's door closed before Mrs. Katzen could see where I'd been.

"Tyler Reynolds!" she said in surprise as she entered. "What do you need?"

"Um..." I slipped the keys quietly into my pocket as I glanced nervously around the office. Then I saw the stickers and markers on the secretary's desk.

"A nametag!" I said, thinking fast. "My baby brother didn't get a nametag. All visitors are supposed to have one," I added virtuously.

Mrs. Katzen smiled. "That's right," she said in a satisfied way. "Even infants need to follow the rules."

I wrote "LEON" on a nametag, and reluctantly left the office.

Deven and I were running to get Ryan and Connor when all four of us collided in the lobby.

"We lost our dad," said Connor, picking himself up off the floor.

"We lost our Dude!" said Deven in a panic.

"Nate is trapped in Ms Grieber's closet!" I explained.

Ryan glanced through the glass door at where Mrs. Katzen sat carefully chewing her diet food right in front of Ms Grieber's office door. "That's not part of the plan," he said, like I didn't know that.

"How do I get Nate out of there?" I demanded. I could hear polite chuckling from the lunchroom, reminding me the principal's speech would be over soon.

Ryan frowned. "There's nothing we can do with Ms Katzen there. We have to get her out of the office—fast!" he said.

Then Connor surprised us. "I've got an idea!" he cried. "Come on, Ryan," he tossed over his shoulder as he ran out the front doors.

Ryan struggled for a minute with following Connor's lead. But he didn't have another plan.

"What are you going to do?" I asked.

Ryan shrugged. "I don't know," he said. "Just be ready to rescue Nate." Then he followed Connor out of the school.

Deven and I waited nervously beside the trophy case. Absently I noticed KSM with a lightning bolt scratched in the fake wood-grain.

The bell rang, and kids swarmed the lobby on their way to lunch recess.

"Hi, Tyler!" said a high voice, making me jump.

I turned to see Jayden and a group of his kindergarten friends staring at me like they were waiting for me to do something exciting...like get expelled or maybe arrested.

"Uh, hi," I answered, waving them on toward the playground and panicking as I realized that Jayden had been at the table with Dad before...

The lunchroom doors opened. Parents who had somewhere to be rushed across the lobby and out the front doors, led by Teresa's mother on her way back to the middle school where she was principal.

The speedy parents were followed into the lobby more slowly by the parents who had nothing better to do with their lives. They chatted amongst themselves and gathered around Ms Grieber when she emerged.

Seeing the principal, Deven began making his pied-billed grebe noise, which sounded like: *"Wowp-wowp-wowp-wowp!"*

His grandmother found him and whacked him on the back.

"I am not surprised this food sticks in your throat," she said, with a nod to Nate's mom. "From now on you must carry lunches that I will pack for you."

"We should make a stand on lunchroom nutrition," Mrs. Howe was saying.

Dad nodded seriously while Leon made

goo-goo faces at a gaggle of girls. It was hard to tell whether the girls were making goo-goo faces too or were just reacting to the food in their own way. I was beginning to be glad I hadn't eaten any of it. I was already sick with worry.

Ms Grieber was towering over the crowd of parents, smiling and shaking hands. But soon she would return to her office, which she would find unlocked, with a Dude in the closet.

I felt a rumble through my feet and briefly hoped for an earthquake. But it was just the half-day kindergarten bus pulling into the school drive. For some reason, the bus came partway around the curve and parked awkwardly at an angle, blocking the rushed parents from leaving the parking lot. A line of cars backed up, idling expectantly behind the bus.

Meanwhile, the group of half-day kinder-garteners hopped around on the sidewalk. Their teacher held them back from leaving the curb and walking the dangerous three extra feet to get on their bus. The bus was supposed to pull up to the curb beside them, but something was blocking its path.

I craned my neck to look between the parents. It was Mr. Maguire's motorcycle, parked in the bus lane!

Connor and Ryan must have moved it. I saw them sneak back in the doors just as Mrs. Katzen came barreling out of the office. Her short legs working like pistons, she burst through the crowd and out the doors.

Ms Grieber and the parents turned to gawk out the front windows as the mighty secretary did battle against the forces of improper parking. This was my chance! While no one was looking, I made a beeline for the principal's office.

"Psst! The coast is clear!" I hissed.

Nate came out of the dark closet and kept watch while I locked first the closet door then Ms Grieber's door.

I slapped the magnet onto the back of the file cabinet, and we exited just in time.

Mrs. Katzen, red-faced with fury, stomped past me into the office. A second later, her voice boomed over the intercom:

"WILL THE OWNER OF THE MOTORCYCLE PARKED IN THE BUS LANE PLEASE MOVE HIS VEHICLE!"

"Sorry, Dad, wherever you are," Connor murmured as Nate and I joined the other Dudes by the trophy case.

Ms Grieber sighed and addressed the parents. "Well," she said, "I'm sure this little traffic jam will be cleared up in no time."

Behind her, through the glass doors, I could see Mr. Maguire approach his motorcycle and circle it, scratching his head. Then he threw a leg over, slid on his helmet, and sped off quickly before Ms Grieber and the parents could stroll outside.

Meanwhile, the Dudes turned the opposite direction and headed toward the playground for what was left of recess.

"Whew!" said Ryan, wiping his forehead. "I hope all that was worth it," he said.

I shook my head. "There was so much stuff, and it was dark..." I began to explain.

But Nate interrupted me. "Actually," he said, "I had plenty of time in the closet to find a way around that difficulty."

We all lounged on the cargo net as Nate told us how he'd remembered that Gina Bertrelli's smartphone had been confiscated only yesterday. He'd found it toward the front of one of the shelves.

"It had enough battery left," Nate explained, "to take a lighted video of each of the shelves in the closet."

Ryan rubbed his hands together.

"Great! Where's the phone?" he said.

"I left it in the closet," Nate answered.

The Dudes groaned. What a time to be absent-minded!

"But I emailed the video to my home computer," Nate assured us. "We can check it after school."

The Dudes cheered!

Impossible mission: piece of cake!

Dudes Babysit

We all went over to Nate's after school. His mom welcomed the Dudes and even made us popcorn—which was just as well since we had all missed lunch.

Mrs. Howe was pleased we were going to watch a video. Ever since we made that Zombie Apocalypse movie last summer, she has tried to encourage Nate toward what she calls "creative expression."

The video of Ms Grieber's closet was not Nate's best camera work. The image was dark and grainy, like footage of the ocean floor taken from a submarine. The camera floated up and down the shelves, revealing images of dust-covered, barely identifiable objects. Strange shapes swept into the glare of Gina's phone light and then back into the shadows as the Dudes sat glued to the computer screen, hoping to spot treasure.

"Ms Grieber's sure been busy," Connor remarked.

I half expected to see a big ball of all the gum that Ms Grieber had collected over the years.

"What's that?" asked Deven.

"A cardboard box, I think," Nate answered. "I needed both hands to hold Gina's phone steady so I didn't open it."

"No markings," said Ryan. "It's too small for the Elephant Gun anyway," he pointed out. "Move on."

"What's that?" Connor asked, pointing to the screen.

"Looks like one of those plastic shoes the girls wear," said Nate.

"Just one? There's a story behind that," I said. "Did Ms Grieber make someone walk home without her shoe?"

"Did Ms Grieber make someone walk home without his hair?!" said Deven, pointing to a Random Noise wig slumped forlornly on the shelf.

There was a lot of Sticky-Snot, which was

not really a surprise.

Sticky Snot is a big, glowing blob of sticky rubbery stuff that looks like, well, something that came out of an alien's nose.

You're supposed to pretend to have a huge sneeze and then throw the glob at the wall or the nearest girl and watch people freak as it clings and oozes. It was the kind of unsophisticated joke toy that was all the rage in the younger grades.

"I should have had some of that for my election speech," said Deven wistfully.

"There sure is a lot of it," said Connor.

"Of course there is," I said. "Who would drag their parents to the principal's office to get their snot out of jail?"

"Move on, Nate," Ryan said. "We've gotta find the Elephant Gun."

Nate speeded up the recording. Hats and caps were the most common items in the closet. Next were the kind of small toys like minifigs and little soldiers that you thought you could keep in your pocket but which always ended up having a battle on your desk during social studies—and getting themselves captured by the teacher.

There was a whole shelf of solar-powered dancing monkeys too. These had been a prize for selling magazines for the school fundraiser. They didn't waste batteries, but they sure played their wacky music loud.

"It's like a monkey prison camp!" said Deven, who, I guess, could sympathize with those who were punished for making annoying sounds.

Besides that, there were calculators and jewelry and mini flashlights and flashing jewelry. (Flash Jewels were kind of a thing with the girls for a while. Mr. Isaak complained that they made him want to have a seizure.)

There were no retainers or bike helmets or band instruments. I guess the parents always managed to reclaim those.

And then we saw what we had been looking for. It was lying on the top shelf. Nate had been holding the camera over his head to get the shot. The video was out of focus, but we could see a long tube of green plastic. Then the camera shook and the green shape slid past and out of sight.

The Dudes groaned.

"If we were using a robot, we could tell it to move in and focus by remote control," Nate lamented.

"Wait. Go back. There! Pause it there!" Ryan ordered.

We all gasped.

There it was. We could see something a little blurred but plain enough—stamped on the end of the fake-wood-grained purple stock—the Foam Dart Company logo.

"It's there," Deven breathed.

"There really is an Elephant Gun in Ms Grieber's closet," said Nate.

"And it's going to be in the auction!" said Connor.

"I wonder whose it was?" I said.

"The important thing is whose it's *going* to be," said Ryan. "Now we've gotta get those Bucks."

It was late afternoon when I got home, and I could tell something was wrong. It was a typical

November day: cold, cloudy, and getting dark, but there were no lights on inside. Besides that, the house was locked.

I went around back and saw the shed was dark too. In the side yard, I found this fake rock we have and opened it to get the extra key to the mudroom door.

"Dad?" I called, stepping through the mudroom and into the kitchen. I tossed the key on the table.

It was spooky. The kitchen was dark, but I could hear the TV. I found Jayden sitting on the couch in the family room, staring at cartoons, which was even spookier.

"Hi Tyler," he said tonelessly as I entered.

"Didn't you hear me calling?" I demanded. "Why didn't you answer?"

"You called Dad," Jayden said. I guess that made sense to a five-year-old. "Dad's not here," he added.

Oops. Right. I was supposed to babysit Jayden after school while Dad went to an interview. What with the mission and all, I had forgotten.

"Uh-oh. Am I in trouble?" I asked.

Jayden shrugged. "Ask mom."

"Mom's here?" I said, surprised. I looked around the dark house. "Where?"

"Upstairs," Jayden said, returning his stare to the TV.

Mom was in her bedroom. She was lying on the floor wrapped in a blanket, the throw-up bucket in reach of her outstretched arm. She must be in bad shape to be letting Jayden watch TV. Then I saw Leon a few feet away in his baby-cage. He was squealing and fussing and stretching one fat little leg through the bars as if trying to reach his mommy.

"Mom?" I said. "You got the flu?"

When she answered with a groan, I knew it was time for me to take over—at least until Dad got home. I went to the bathroom and got a wet wash cloth and put it on her forehead like she always did for me when I was sick.

"Tyler," she whispered, rolling slightly and peering at me from under the cloth.

"It's okay, Mom," I said quickly. "You rest."

"Leon..." she mumbled.

"I got him," I insisted. I went to the baby-cage and hefted my baby brother over my shoulder.

Mom pointed to the phone where it lay on the floor beside her, so I picked it up. "Help..." she began.

"Don't worry, Mom. I'm taking over. Tyler to the rescue!"

I went downstairs and set Leon on his belly on the rug in front of the TV. Then I took the phone to the kitchen to call for back-up. When I returned, I found Leon on his back with a Lego man in his slobbery hand.

"Hey! When did you learn to roll over?" I said, swooping down to snatch the toy before it could go in the slobbery baby mouth.

"He's not allowed to have this stuff. He could swallow it!" I shouted at Jayden, who looked up from the TV—surprised but not particularly concerned.

"Hi Leon," he said, before returning his stare to the screen.

"Great," I said, hoisting Leon off the floor. Jayden wasn't gonna be any help.

Luckily, the cavalry was on its way in the form of Ryan, Connor, Deven and Nate.

"Dude, I don't know anything about babies," Deven said when they arrived. "My sister is seventeen."

(Actually, Shaila was *our* babysitter on the rare occasions she could find time between debate team, Junior Symphony, and Medical Careers Club.)

"I don't have any experience either," Nate admitted.

"It's no big deal, guys," I assured them. "I know all the rules from when Shaila babysits." Then I ticked them off on my fingers: "Don't open the door to strangers. Don't let the baby have stuff he could choke on. And don't let Jayden watch TV."

We all looked over to where Jayden was now lying upside down watching a toy commercial with his feet up the back of the couch and his head hanging over the front.

"Um, I guess this is an emergency," I said.

"Just keep Leon entertained while I get us some food, okay? I'm starving."

"Me too!" said Connor, following me into the kitchen.

I got out a box of crackers and a package of string cheese.

Connor got out the peanut butter and the raspberry jelly and a jar of pickles and leftover salsa and a bag of tortillas and some grapes.

Ryan, Deven, and Nate came into the kitchen with the baby. Actually, Ryan flew Leon into the kitchen like a pudgy airplane. Leon was squealing with delight.

Connor turned to look, dripping some jelly out of his tortilla. "You guys want a snack?" he offered.

"I don't know. What do you have?" Ryan asked, handing the baby off to Deven, whose knees buckled.

"Whoa! This kid's heavy," he complained.

"Lift with your legs," Nate suggested.

"Huh?" said Deven, raising one foot off the floor and giving it a puzzled look.

Nate took Leon and put him in his high chair. Just then, the doorbell rang.

I had finally gotten my string cheese open, so I said to Connor, "Go see who it is, will ya?"

He stuffed the rest of his tortilla in his mouth and left the room. He came running back with wide eyes.

"It's a stranger!" said Connor, spewing chewed tortilla across the kitchen.

Ryan pulled his head out of the fridge. "No biggee," he said. "Just don't answer it."

Connor looked at me, and I nodded. "That's the rule," I said.

"Did he see you?" asked Nate.

"I don't think so," said Connor fishing for a pickle with his fingers. "I looked through that little window at the top of the door."

"Probably a salesman," I said.

Just then, a loud knocking sound came from the front door.

"Shh!" said Ryan. "He'll think there's no one home and go away in a minute."

We all waited—and chewed—silently.

I saw Leon open his mouth, so I quickly shoved in a spoonful of jelly. I had experience with little brothers, you know.

After a while, we kinda relaxed.

"Go take a look," Ryan ordered Connor. "See if he's gone."

Connor came back more freaked out than before. "He's still here!" he hissed. "He's gotta be! His truck's still in the driveway, but I can't see him anywhere."

We all instinctively looked to Ryan for orders. Fending off invasion by hostile forces was kinda his thing.

Ryan's eyes narrowed. "Okay. We need to get eyes on him," he said. "Fan out, everyone. Check from all the windows, and report back here. And guys," he added. "ninja stealth *on*!"

I started to leave the kitchen with the others, but Leon's about-to-wail face stopped me.

"Don't worry, little guy. I won't leave you," I said. I'd just pried him out of the highchair when the guys came back.

"The stranger is outside the mudroom

door!" Deven reported with a little salute.

"If he believes no one is home, he may be looking for a way in," suggested Nate.

"Dude! He's casing the joint!" said Connor.

Ryan elbowed him and asked, "Could you see what he was doing, Dev?"

Deven shrugged. "Looking around in the flowerbed, kicking the dirt and stuff," he said.

"Probably looking for a rock to smash the window," suggested Nate.

I held Leon tighter. "We've gotta do something!" I said.

"All right!" said Ryan, holding up his hands. "First, Connor, keep an eye on this guy," he held up two fingers to his eyes and added, "like a ninja."

Connor nodded and slipped silently out of the kitchen, hugging the wall.

Ryan turned to the rest of us. "Next thing we've got to do is get the little guys to safety. Tyler, you take Jayden and Leon out the back door and make a run for it."

"No way," I answered, shaking my head. "My mother's sick upstairs. I can't leave her alone."

Ryan seemed to understand my logic.

"Okay," he said. "Deven and Nate will take the kids."

He turned to them. "You're on a mission, guys," Ryan said. "Go to the nearest neighbor that's home and call the police."

Connor crawled back through the door from the dining room. "He's in the front yard again," he said.

"Is he leaving?" I asked, half-hoping this was all a mistake.

But Connor shook his head. "He had his cell phone out. Do you think he's calling in his gang?"

"Now's your chance," said Ryan. He slung the diaper bag around Deven's neck as Deven staggered toward the deck door, carrying Leon under his arm sideways like a football. Meanwhile, Nate was literally dragging Jayden from the couch.

"Get going," Ryan hissed, sliding the back door open for them. "We'll hold him off 'til the police come."

A gust of cold air took my breath away and ruffled Ryan's hair. There was a gleam in his eye—

the same gleam in the eye of every tough action hero who's ever been one of the good guys. At that moment, I was proud to be on his team.

Jayden kept giggling and twisting. Luckily, he was wearing socks, so Nate was able to skid him across the hardwood and out the door to the deck.

It gets dark early in November. I hoped the twilight would cover their escape. Unfortunately, Jayden squealed when he finally lost sight of the TV.

Connor came rushing into the kitchen. "He heard that!" he said. He's coming!"

Dudes Defense

"He knows we're here now," said Ryan, locking the deck door. "We need a new plan."

That's when we heard the front doorknob jiggle. The burglar was definitely trying to get in.

"What if he can pick the lock?" I asked. "I wish we had an alarm or something."

"That's it!" said Ryan. "Time for Operation Noise Barrier! You guys make as much noise as you can to try to scare him away. Then meet me in Tyler's room."

Ryan disappeared down the basement stairs.

Connor and I shuffled through the house, keeping low under the windows and creeping around doorframes.

That same toy commercial was on TV again, so we turned up the volume.

I turned on my dad's speakers too. He'd been listening to an audiobook, so this woman's voice boomed out, talking about how to save time with a slow cooker. I wished Dad was into something that sounded a little more intimidating, but at least the woman was enthusiastic.

Upstairs, Connor turned up the CD player in Jayden's room and a bunch of screechy little kids started belting out songs about trains and spiders. If that didn't scare the guy, nothing would.

Ryan joined us in my room. He had a bundle under his arm. "The gang's arrived," he reported. "I saw at least two more guys in dark clothes with flashlights.

"The noise didn't scare them, but it sure made them curious," he added. "They're peeking in all the downstairs windows."

"If only we had an anvil or something to drop on their heads," said Connor.

"An anvil," I said, "like in a cartoon?"

"Well, something heavy," Connor replied. He hefted my souvenir geode in one hand.

"Too risky," said Ryan, grabbing the round

rock and setting it back on my chest of drawers.
"What if you miss?"

"I'm the best pitcher on the baseball team,"
said Connor, puffing up his chest.

"And you still walked like seven hundred
guys last season," Ryan pointed out.

"We don't have time to fight," I said.

Ryan shook his head. "We may *have* to
fight if those guys get in here," he said. "Better find
some weapons."

All our dart guns were in the treehouse.
And, over the summer while she was home with
us all day, Mom had gotten rid of everything in the
house with which Jayden and I could possibly hit
each other.

My only hope was the laundry room cabinet. On the top shelf, Mom keeps stuff that's off
limits because it's dangerous or messy or annoying
to grownups. I climbed up on the washer to take a
look.

Inside I found several permanent markers,
the missing caps from Jayden's cap gun, the superhero whose body armor was always falling off, and

three eggs of silly putty. (My mom was kind of paranoid about silly putty getting on the carpet, but I didn't think it would scare a burglar.)

Then I saw something else. "Bingo!" I said, grabbing two cans of spray string and heading back across the hall.

"I got something," I said as I returned to my room.

"Me too," said Ryan. He unrolled his bundle to reveal our old volleyball net. "This ought to snare one of them until the police come."

"Dudes!" Connor hissed from where he was looking out the window. "They're on the deck."

I could barely see two men creeping around below us. Their clothes were dark, and their faces were hidden by hats.

Luckily, Granddad took all the screens off the windows a few weeks ago, so we had clear access to fire. They must have heard us opening the window, though, because the big guy looked up just as Ryan tossed the net.

Ryan gave it a good fling so it didn't land in a lump but kind of spread out over the burglar's head. Then Connor and I let the second guy have it with the spray string.

It wasn't until about the time I ran out of neon green string that I noticed the silver badge on the second guy's shirt.

Connor stopped spraying neon orange and dropped the can on my foot.

Ryan gulped.

With effort, the first guy—Officer Morgan of the Sherwood Police—peeled the net off his head and shined his flashlight up at us.

"All right, boys," he called. "I think you'd better come out here."

When we stepped out the front door into the blustery night, the first thing I saw was Grandad's pick-up in the driveway.

He rushed forward as we came out of the house. "Tyler! I'm glad you're all right," Granddad said. He grabbed me in a quick hug then asked, "Where are Meg and Jayden and the baby?"

Just then Jayden tackled Granddad from

behind, nearly knocking him over.

"We were hiding from the burglar, Grand-dad," he explained.

"Then there *was* a burglar!" said Granddad. "I *thought* I saw someone sneaking around that house. I'm glad I called the police."

Uh-oh.

Granddad said, "I even saw someone run out the back carrying a heavy sack of loot."

"That was Leon," Jayden told him.

Grandad looked a little confused, but I was beginning to get the picture.

Deven and Nate had gathered around too, by this time, along with Mrs. Kostenko who was carrying Leon.

"Did they catch the burglar?" she asked Granddad.

He shrugged.

"This is a job for Batman," Jayden informed her.

Then Dad got home from work. He had to park in the street because the police car was block-ing the driveway. He blinked in the flashing lights and then gave a puzzled frown at all of us standing around in the yard.

It was about that time that Officer Morgan came limping around from the side yard. He approached Dad with an angry look, asking, "Sir, can you explain why you have a hole in your yard big enough to bury a body?"

(Oops. Guess we should have filled it in again after we dug up Connor's Sushiraser.)

It turned out that Mom had come home sick from work. When Dad left for his interview, she had called Granddad to come help with the baby.

It was Granddad who had come to the front door and who had searched for the side door key— which was no longer in the fake rock because I'd left it on the kitchen table. I realized that I'd never actually seen the burglar, though he'd been clear in my imagination after Connor saw a "stranger".

When Granddad had spotted Connor sneaking around in the house, he had called the police.

Mrs. Kostenko had too, when Deven and Nate arrived. And she'd changed Leon's diaper, which was also pretty urgent.

Mom, of course, had heard only the loud music, and, being too sick to come tell me to turn it off, had lain there thinking I was a noisy jerk instead of a hero. I would have been in trouble, except she now realized how I was trying to defend her.

When everything was sorted out, the older policeman handed the volleyball net to Dad, who tried to ignore that the officer's hair was still sticking out at the side and his pants were muddy from where he'd fallen in the zombie hole in the dark.

"I'm sorry about all this," Dad said sheepishly. "The boys seem to have let their imaginations run away with them."

He glared our direction, and the Dudes all tried to look as innocent as we could.

"Better safe than sorry," said Officer Morgan wearily.

"Right!" put in the younger policeman whose name was Racarro. "You know it was only a few months ago that we chased some cat burglars out of this neighborhood."

"*Cat* burglars?" repeated Jayden, his eyes

wide. I could tell he was imagining actual cats committing crimes. (Of course, I wasn't going to set him straight on who the police had *really* been chasing last summer, but I figured the Dudes could take it as a compliment on our ninja stealth.)

Officer Morgan sighed as he peeled some neon green string off the side of his partner's face. "Next time, boys," he advised, "let the *police* use the dangerous weapons."

As the officers left, Dad turned to Deven, Nate, Ryan, and Connor. He looked a little pale, which might have been the effect of trying to explain the Dudes to the police. Or maybe it was the flu coming on.

"You'd better go home now, boys," he said, adding hesitantly, "and, um, thank you for helping out."

"Think nothing of it, Mr. Reynolds," Ryan responded. "Call on the Dudes anytime for your babysitting needs!"

 # *Downhill Dudes*

Winter break was awesome, as any three weeks without school would be—especially since Mom was at work, so no one was keeping track of screen time!

Dad had finished his shelves and built himself a desk out of two filing cabinets and an old closet door. Then he carted a bunch of baby toys to the shed so Leon wouldn't be bored watching Dad sit around waiting for a client.

"You'll need more insulation," Granddad said at Christmas dinner.

"I'll wear a sweater," Dad answered.

"You're out of a job. I don't want you to get pneumonia too," Granddad warned.

Dad said he wasn't "out of a job" he had *quit* his job. He didn't explain the difference though.

Deven didn't want Sensei to get pneumonia

122

either. Sensei was a plaster garden gnome that usually inhabited our treehouse dojo. When the weather got cold, Deven brought him inside to keep warm.

"My mom had flowerpots that cracked in freezing weather," Connor informed us, causing Deven to cover Sensei's ears.

The Dudes' usual winter habitat is my basement. It's where we play Legos and have dart gun battles and expose ourselves to the dangers of screen time playing video games.

This year, Jayden, Leon and I each got a set of cardboard bricks for Christmas. (Leon was too small to play with them yet, but at least he couldn't swallow them!) Our three sets together added up to a lot of bricks which the Dudes used to build a temple for Sensei so he could watch over us while we thought up awesome plans.

Listening Bear watched us too. (Jayden's turn to bring home the Kindergarten teddy bear fell on winter break.) Listening Bear is supposed to go where you go and do what you do, and then you have to write it all down in his little notebook for the class to read.

It sounded like some kind of home surveillance plan to me. But Jayden loved it and wrote something every day while school was out.

Mostly he wrote about the Dudes' holiday activities:

- like when we turned off the lights in the basement and had a night battle with Mom's battery-operated decorative candy canes
- or when we dubbed Santa hats and "Ho-ho-ho's" into the zombie apocalypse movie we made last summer
- or when we taped jingle bells to our bikes and played Wheels of War in the dark cul-de-sac at midnight on New Year's Eve.

I didn't mind helping the little guy with spelling. I was sort of proud that Jayden was writing about the Dudes just like his big brother. Maybe someday I'll even let him read the Chronicles...

I mean, when he's older...lots older. Anyway, having to write in Listening Bear's journal kind of makes up for how Jayden usually has no homework and gets to spend his time reading comic books, while I have to slave away to earn homework bucks.

Speaking of homework, the Dudes were all dreading the start of school after the New Year. Luckily, at the end of break, Mother Nature dumped a miracle on us in the form of six inches of snow overnight!

Jayden and I got up early to enjoy the snow day. Leon always gets up early, so Mom was up too. When she found out she was snowed in she made pancakes and took pictures of us in our snow pants and got all mushy like it was the last time she was gonna see our noses running or something.

Dad was more cheerful. "This is the beauty of working at home," he said, gesturing with his coffee cup. "I can always get to the office." But, after a half hour in the shed, he was back inside.

"I wish that snowplow would come through," Dad said. "I've got to get out to buy some insulation and a space heater."

Jayden and I didn't mind the cold. First thing, Jayden scooped up a snowball and brought it inside.

"You gotta save this for Leon until he's older," Jayden told Mom.

Mom smiled. "Okay," she said. "I'll put it in the freezer, where it will be nice and safe."

I had to wait while Jayden checked that the snowball was nestled happily against a carton of ice cream. Then we went out again.

First, we stabbed each other with some icicle swords we found hanging off the gutter. Then we walked around the neighborhood. As we walked, Jayden kept scooping up snow in his mittens and eating it. The neighborhood was all white and sparkly. And, other than Jayden occasionally saying, "Mmmm, good!" it was quieter than usual—like the snow muffled everything. At least until we got in sight of Deven's house.

He was drawing goofy faces in the frost on his dad's car. When he saw us coming, he cupped his hands around his mouth and shouted "Du-uuuude! No schoooool!" so loudly that clumps of snow fell off the branches of the cherry trees in his yard. Some plopped onto his head, taking some of the height out of his Random Noise hair—which Deven was wearing instead of a hat.

The sound must have carried because it was only about a minute later that Nate walked over, carrying a cup of hot cocoa. It steamed as he poured it over Jayden's snowball. We were hoping for a chocolate snowcone, but it really just made muddy-looking water that soaked into Jayden's mittens.

Luckily, about that time Deven's grand-mother invited us all inside for cocoa. While we drank, she put Jayden's mittens in the washer and brought out one of Deven's old pairs to loan him.

"Thanks," said Jayden, with a chocolate mustache.

When we were finished there, we headed over to Ryan and Connor's place. They were out front having a snowball fight. The snow was just right—wet enough to stick together and pack down hard to make good projectiles.

Mrs. Maguire invited us in for hot cocoa too. I was beginning to think there was some kind of parental conspiracy—or maybe there had been a sale on cocoa last week.

When she left the room, Connor whispered, "Dad's got a girlfriend."

I looked at Ryan, who nodded. "We met her last weekend," he said. "Connor doesn't like her."

"I like Mom," Connor grumbled.

Ryan shrugged. "Tina's cool," he said.

"Tina's lame," Connor shot back, his fist clenching around his cocoa.

I was beginning to see why they were fighting when we arrived.

"Tina's okay," Ryan said, with a wary glance at Connor. "Besides, Dad can't help it if girls like him. That's how it is with us cool guys."

Nate and I looked at each other. You had to admire his confidence.

We finished the cocoa and went back outside. Nate analyzed the two snow forts Ryan and Connor had built.

"Using offset brick technique with the giant snowballs was a good call," he said.

"Thanks," said Ryan. "Dad showed us that last winter."

"*Before* he met Tina," grumbled Connor.

"How did you make those giant snowballs?" Jayden asked. I hoped he wasn't thinking of eating one.

"I'll show you, little Dude," said Ryan. "First you make a regular snowball. Then you find some good snow to roll it in." He looked around their yard, but there wasn't much snow left.

I could read the footprints like a record of their earlier battle: The two forts, the sneak attack, the retreat through the side yard, the ambush under the lilac bush, the skirmish by the front steps...

"Uh, let's go over to your house where there's better snow," suggested Ryan.

Of course, Jayden ate his snowball on the way over, but there was still lots to work with at our house. It really was cool how you could roll a snowball and it would get bigger and bigger until you couldn't push it anymore—just like in a cartoon. It made this great crunching sound as it rolled too.

"I'm gonna make the biggest snowman!" Jayden said. But after making the first ball he got tired and left it by the shed in order to go in for, guess what? Hot cocoa.

I guess, with all that snow in his stomach, the little guy needed the heat. But the rest of us had had enough cocoa. Besides, a snow day was too good an opportunity to waste.

"Dad says the school Superintendent makes the decision to call off school for the whole city," Ryan told us. "When there's bad weather, the radio and tv and everybody find out from that one guy."

I sensed a story coming on, and I wasn't wrong.

"Anyway," Ryan explained, "when Dad was a kid, the superintendent happened to live at the end of a dead end street. One time when they had a snow day, Dad and his friends collected all the snow from all their yards and went over at night and put it on the street in front of the Superintendent's house while he was sleeping."

Ryan glanced around to see if we were getting the picture.

"In the morning, the guy looked out and saw snow again and called off school. Dad's crew gave the whole district an extra snow day!"

"Not bad!" said Deven.

But Nate said, "It seems they spent their first snow day working in order to create a second snow day."

"At least they weren't stupid enough to spend it with a girlfriend," sniped Connor.

"Dad's not stupid," said Ryan, his gloves curling into fists.

"Look, guys, we've got a snow day here," I broke in, hoping to change the subject. "How are we going to spend it?"

"Let's go skiing—or at least sledding," said Connor.

"Where?" asked Nate. "We don't have a good hill for sledding."

"Yeah. For a place called Sherwood Heights, our neighborhood is pretty flat," Deven agreed.

"Every neighborhood should have a good sledding hill," I said. "It's like a civic responsibility."

"Dudes!" said Ryan suddenly. "If we don't have one, we gotta build it ourselves!"

"Huh?" said Deven.

"Out of what?" Connor asked.

Ryan patted Jayden's big snowball. "We've got all the materials we need!" he said.

We got down to it right away, rolling all the snow from the front and back yards into balls that we could pile up against Jayden's.

When we heard the snow plow coming, it was Nate's idea to lay all our sleds on the sidewalk. The snow was dirty, but we caught tons of it as the plow threw it off the street.

"Mush! Mush!" Deven yelled, pushing while Nate pulled the heavy sleds to the back yard.

By the time Dad came out, we had already moved all the snow in the front yard to the back.

"Thanks for clearing the driveway, boys!" he called with a wave as he backed the car out of the garage.

Meanwhile, in the backyard, we used shovels and buckets to pile the snow on top of the mountain. Then we got the ladder out of the garage and piled it even higher.

Everyone took breaks in shifts to go home

for lunch. And, when they came back, they brought snow from their own yards. Then the dudes went around the neighborhood, ringing doorbells and asking to clear driveways. When other kids found out what we were doing, they pitched in to haul back the loads of snow. After all, the sledding hill was going to be a community resource!

It doesn't take as long to build a mountain as you might think. By mid-afternoon, Operation Everest was living up to its name. Nate actually had to cut steps on one side of the snow hill so we could climb to the top of the run like mountain climbers.

There was a long line of kids waiting to try it out. But the Dudes got to go first. Of course, Connor had his own way of getting to the top.

"Look, Dudes! A ski lift!" he shouted, reaching for the handle of the Flying Kick. Connor flew through the air. When he reached the top of the mountain, he dropped from the zip-line to his sled and glided down the run.

Nate gave him high marks for technical difficulty as well as style points for his splashy dismount when the sled planted its nose in the nearly bare grass at the bottom of the hill and flipped over, face-planting Connor in the yard.

Yeah. The hill was a little steep. We must have gotten carried away piling more snow on top than we did on the sides. No problem. We just had to refine our sledding technique. Once we learned how to catch ourselves with our feet instead of our faces we were in business.

We tried different ways of sliding and did stunts for a while. Then we made up some Olympics-style sports like bobsled biathlon—in which you had to shoot at a flying Frisbee with a dart gun on the way down.

It got dark early, and the other kids had all gone home by the time the Dudes and I finally went in my house for one more mug of hot cocoa. We were sucking marshmallows through our teeth when Dad got home with a bunch of stuff from the hardware store.

"Supper won't be for an hour," Mom warned him.

"Good," Dad said. "I'm going to go out and

get started with the insulation."

Dad went out the back door and came back a minute later with a wild look on his face.

"Who," he said, glancing around the table at the Dudes, "buried my office under a mountain of snow?!"

The Dudes looked at each other. We hadn't really noticed that we were piling the snow on the shed, but, come to think of it, that did explain how the mountain could have gotten so high so quickly.

"On the plus side," offered Nate, "snow is an excellent insulator."

"But I can't get in!" Dad shouted. (I guess that was the minus side.)

Of course, Ryan had a solution.

"Don't worry, Mr. Reynolds, he said. "We can dig you a tunnel!"

I think taking a snow tunnel to work would be epic, but Dad seemed to doubt the Dudes' engineering expertise. He made us spend our second snow day shoveling all our hard-earned snow away from the shed so the meltwater wouldn't rot the walls or flood the foundations.

It was actually a nice change of pace. Ryan brought over his hatchet and ski goggles and chopped like a madman until the packed snow was in chunks. Nate directed the rest of us in turning the chunks of snow into a giant snow fort! When kids came over looking for the sledding hill, Ryan grouped them into squads to attack the defenses.

After a day of that going on right outside his office, though, Dad was anxious for the Dudes to go back to school. And when we finally did, Deven had this announcement:

Good Morning, Sherwood Students!

Hope you made the most of your snow days!

I have an announcement from Tyler Reynolds: After an explosion took out the defenders' right flank and everyone fell back for rations, someone in the attacking force left a retainer on the battlefield. This means you, Squad B!

The soldier in question can pick up his retainer in the office.

Dudes Dilemma

Happy Valentine's Day, Sherwood Seals.

Ms Grieber would like me to announce that class parties will be held during the last hour of the day. Please stay out of love—and candy—until then.

Music in the lunchroom today will be Troy Diamond singing "Heart in a Cage".

Today's inspirational message is: Whoever's got Troy Diamond's heart in a cage, please give it back! The guy sounds like he's dying!

The weirdness started at recess. There we were playing kickball, with two outs and a man on first when Ryan caught the ball and suddenly whirled and threw it at Teresa, who was not even part of the game!

Teresa was standing there talking to her friend, Melanie, when the kickball came out of nowhere and bopped her on the back of the head. She looked around kind of annoyed with her ponytail askew.

And (here's where it gets weird) Ryan yelled, "Hi Teresa!" with this big goofy grin on his face.

Teresa just rolled her eyes and turned back to Melanie. (Of course, being Teresa, she didn't do the polite thing and return the ball.)

That afternoon, after the class party, I noticed Ryan going through all his valentines actually *reading* the names instead of just ripping off the candy that was taped to them. This was weird too, but I didn't connect it with the kickball thing until a week later.

That Saturday we were all in my basement working on a game we called Instant Obliteration: Survival Mode. It was inspired by school, and it was sort of like a real life video game. The player had to hop over things and roll under things and break through walls. We were using hula hoops and broomsticks and cardboard bricks to make the obstacles.

The mission was to rescue Sensei, who was currently imprisoned in an old cat carrier Jayden had bought at a yard sale in the hopes of convincing Mom to get a pet. We had planned to put him in a cave (Sensei, not Jayden). But our cave was the closet under the stairs, and Ryan vetoed that idea on account of possible spiders. So Sensei's jail was perched on the shelf over the TV where he was safe. (We don't shoot toward the TV because the darts leave little sucker marks on the screen.)

Jayden wanted to help, so he was sitting on the stairs above Sensei's shelf, acting as the enemy sniper. It was only since Christmas that the little guy's fingers got strong enough to cock the Dominator, and now there's nothing he likes better than pulling that trigger over and over. With Jayden keeping up a steady stream of fire from the top of the basement stairs, no one had made it through alive yet. That's why we were still modifying the game.

Nate had made some cardboard armor. That gave you three hits before you lost a life token.

Ryan was working on a helmet too.

And Connor had another idea. "If you break through this wall here," he said, demonstrating by knocking down the bricks, "you'll find a weapon you can use to pick off the sniper."

Connor picked up the Recon Rifle from where it had been hidden. "I'm gonna hide extra ammo around too," he added.

While he was talking, my little brother shot him in the chest three times.

"You're dead!" yelled Jayden from the stairs.

Connor shrugged and told us, "That's what makes it a challenge."

"You'd better find plenty of extra Life Tokens," said Deven, holding up one of the plastic cupcakes from our pretend kitchen. We had hidden a bunch of cupcakes around the basement too.

Nate was thinking (as always). "If I *build* a robot instead of buying one," he said, "I could add bullet-proof armor and write a program to seek out hidden ammo."

I wasn't sure it would be fair for Nate to use a robot on his turn. But he *had* donated his robot money to buy a case of Sushirasers. I looked to Ryan for a ruling and was surprised to see him leaving.

"Where are you going?" I asked.

"Mom said to come home early so she can cut my hair," said Ryan. "Gotta look good for my date tomorrow."

"Huh?" said Deven.

I must have heard that wrong. "I thought you were going to Teresa's party tomorrow," I said.

Teresa had invited the whole fifth grade to her birthday party at the trampoline place. A lot of the boys weren't going, but Ryan always said, "You can't let a little thing like a girl get in the way of two hours on a trampoline." Of course, that had been when he was in his right mind...

Now Ryan smiled. "Of course I'm going to Teresa's party," he answered. "She's my girlfriend."

"What?" I said.

I looked at Nate and saw him rubbing his glasses like his eyes couldn't believe what his ears had heard.

"You're dating Teresa?" he asked.

"*Terrible* Teresa?" I added, in case there was any confusion.

Ryan shrugged. "I need a girlfriend, so, who

else?"

He had me there.

Ryan chuckled at the look on my face.

"You'll understand the appeal someday, kid," he said. Then he sauntered upstairs in his cardboard armor and his aluminum foil helmet.

"That's just what Dad said when he told us about his girlfriend, Tina," said Connor mournfully.

Deven's reaction was more dramatic.

"Ryan's lost his mind!" he screeched. He looked to where Sensei peered out of the cat carrier, his expression mysterious behind his long white beard.

"Sensei," Deven called, "You'll have to take command."

After Ryan left, Nate and I sat on the steps in shock. Across from us, Connor and Deven were letting Jayden shoot them each in the forehead and comparing how far the darts bounced to see who had the most rubbery skull.

After watching that for a while, Nate said, "You know, Ryan is the most mature of all of us."

It was true. Ryan had been born seven minutes before Connor, and they were both three months older than me. After me came Deven and then Nate.

"So what?" I asked.

Nate's face was serious. "It's possible his fate is an inevitable pitfall of aging," he answered.

"Great. Shoot me now," I moaned.

So Jayden did.

The next day, at the party, I asked Connor what was going on.

Connor did a couple somersaults in mid-air (to spin blood to his brain, I guess).

"I bet it's because of the big heart-shaped box of chocolates Dad got Tina for Valentine's Day," he said when he was right-side-up again. "Even though he gave it to *her*, they shared it while they watched videos—so Dad ended up getting half!"

Connor seemed confident, but I wasn't sure. "We all like chocolate," I said, "but what does Ryan want with a girlfriend?"

Connor bounced off the wall and came back.

"Just to have one, I guess, like Dad." He sighed heavily. "It's all Tina's fault," he added.

I looked around. At the party, the boys and girls were keeping their natural distance from each other—all except Ryan. On the other side of the gym, Ryan was letting a bunch of girls gang up on him in trampoline dodge ball.

"Maybe he's gonna hit Teresa in the *face* with the ball this time," guessed Deven.

I plummeted into the foam pit. Nate caromed off the nearest wall and landed clumsily beside me. He was wearing green-tinted prescription goggles that made him look like some kind of space bug.

"Maybe we should try to snap Ryan out of it," suggested the space bug. "For Teresa's sake as well as our own."

"How do we do that?" I asked, dragging myself across the foam.

"We could give him something bad to smell every time he sees Teresa," Connor suggested, sailing over our heads as Nate and I climbed out of the pit.

"Connor's socks ought to do it," Deven put in. He was springing high on the big tramp. Every time he reached the high point, he froze in a different silly cartoon-like position in mid-air—you know:

I just got hit by an anvil!

bounce

I just ran through a wall!

bounce

I just smelled Connor's socks!

Connor tried to help him with that last one by showing off the flying dragon kick he learned in P.E. last week.

As Connor's foot collided with Deven's face, Nate shook his head. "I think following Ryan around with something emitting noxious fumes would be impractical," he said.

"And it might not work," I pointed out. "I mean, if Teresa being herself hasn't turned him off..."

"I know!" said Connor, untangling himself

from Deven. "We could hit Ryan on the head to see if he comes out of it."

"That's for amnesia," I said.

"If *we* don't do it, *Teresa* will," he warned. "Did you see how she pulverized the padded dummy in P.E. last week?"

"Yeah," put in Deven. "And Ryan's a dummy *without* pads!"

"Perhaps hypnosis would work," mused Nate, gazing through green-tinted goggles. "I've always wanted to try it."

"Ooo! You could make Ryan cluck like a chicken!" Deven suggested, flapping his wings.

Just then, I noticed Mrs. Gutierrez frowning in our direction. I thought she might not like the way the Dudes were keeping our distance from the girls—or acting like barnyard fowl. But she just clapped her hands and directed us all to the snack bar where there were circular tables on a polka dot rug. I don't know if round food was mandatory, but they did serve us pepperoni pizza and cupcakes.

The girls all bunched around one table and the boys around the other.

At the boys' table, Connor's cheeks were flushed, either with excitement or because he was leaning over the steaming cheese.

"I know!" he whispered. "Let's start up an anti-girls club and tell Ryan he can't be in it unless he gives up his girlfriend."

We all looked over to where Teresa was giving Ryan dirty looks because he was squeezing in between her and Melanie at the girls' table. There was just no way to be sure, in Ryan's state of confusion, that he would make the right choice.

"I don't want to have a club without Ryan," I said.

"Me either," admitted Deven.

"The Dudes stick together no matter what," said Nate.

Finally, Connor agreed.

I raised my cupcake and the other guys raised theirs.

"If Ryan wants a girlfriend," I said, "then the Dudes will make it our mission to get him one."

"Yeah!" grunted the guys.

Then we stuffed our faces.

Dudes in Love

When it came to making Teresa his girl-friend, Ryan really *did* need help. Hitting her with a ball hadn't worked. Neither had grossing out her friends by snorting soda through his nose at her party. And she hadn't said anything about the Ninja Wars valentine he gave her. (She had given him one that had a little dog with big eyes saying "Woof is in the air.") It didn't seem like a good sign.

On Monday, Ryan walked over to Teresa's house after school. Teresa's yard had a buried wire all the way around it. Her dog, Teacup, wore a little collar that zapped him if he stepped over the wire. Ryan's plan was to hang around (just outside the invisible fence). Naturally, Teacup would come tearing out. Ryan hoped Teresa would either come out to collect her maniacal dog or at least look out to see if the Chihuahua had killed anyone.

While Ryan was gone, the rest of the Dudes had a meeting at my house to discuss Operation Woo (Yeah, Deven named this one.)

I told the guys, "The problem is Teresa doesn't seem to *know* she's supposed to be Ryan's girlfriend."

"Maybe Ryan needs to do more than get her attention," said Nate. "Maybe he needs to be romantic."

I gulped. "You mean like serenade under her window?" I asked.

Deven's fist shot into the air. "Hooooot!" he hooted.

"No," said Nate hastily. "I don't think that will help."

"Bring her flowers?" I said.

"It's February," Connor pointed out. "There's nothing to pick out of anyone's yard."

"What else do girls like?" I wondered. "I mean besides Sushirasers." (The girls had already snapped up all the Sushirasers we'd bought using Nate's robot money.)

Deven suggested writing Teresa a poem.

Then he really surprised us by pulling his hand out of his pocket and reciting one:

My love, only you call me so fine.

Let's kiss, whatever, I'm yours, be mine.

"Dude! How did you make that up?" asked Connor with admiration.

"And why does it sound familiar?" asked Nate with suspicion.

Deven flashed his teeth in a grin. "It's from the words on candy hearts," he explained. "I couldn't work in 'LOL' so I ate that one."

He held out his hand with the battered candies in it. "We could write it down and put Ryan's name on it," he offered.

But Nate shook his head. "I don't think we should put anything in writing," he said, "in case Ryan comes to his senses later."

The Dudes were out of ideas and desperate, so I decided to ask Dad. I found him in the shed arguing with Granddad.

"If you've got time on your hands…" Granddad was saying.

"I don't, Dad. I'm going to get a client any

day now!"

"I understand, son. But it wouldn't take long to put storm windows in those screen frames I made."

"Dad, thanks, but I don't need...Oh! Hi, Tyler," said Dad. He seemed *way* too glad to see me.

I laid out Ryan's problem for the both of them.

"I would advise Ryan to wait until he's at least twelve to tie himself down," Dad joked. (This is the kind of help you get from parents.)

Then he stared into space. "I remember when I first got interested in your mother in college," Dad said. "I overheard that she was having a hard time finding a book for her history class. The campus store didn't have it, so I biked across town to find one for her."

I had to ask the obvious: "Why didn't she just order it online?"

Dad looked at Granddad, and they both chuckled. Guess I fixed *their* problem.

Dad said, "The point is Ryan should show Teresa that he's thought about what she likes."

I thought about what Teresa likes: ballet, telling people what to do, not getting hit in the head with balls. I wasn't sure there was a gift in there.

Then Granddad said, "In the old days, boys used to carve the girl's initials on a tree."

"But people don't do that anymore," Dad jumped in urgently. "Ryan should *not carve anything!*"

That gave me an idea, though. I had seen lots of girls write that plus sign with their initials and the initials of Troy Diamond or the guy from Vampire Musical.

Girls usually wrote those things on a notebook or even on their hand. But, when I mentioned it, Ryan had a bigger and better idea.

Friday after school, Ryan sprayed RM + TG in four-foot-tall wiggly pink neon letters across Teresa's front yard. (Luckily, we had enough silly string left over after spraying the police in November.)

Nate suggested that he surround the whole thing with a giant heart, but Ryan didn't want to get too mushy.

"Wait'll Teresa comes out and sees that," Ryan said proudly. "I happen to know she's got ballet class in a few minutes."

The dudes scrambled. There was a line of rhododendrons beside Teresa's driveway that hid us pretty well and made a perfect spot from which to watch.

Sure enough, about a minute later, a member of the Gutierrez family came outside. But it was Teacup. He came trotting out his little doggy door to do his business, I guess. When he saw the silly string, he stopped in his tracks. Then he went sniffing all around until he found the spot on the sidewalk where Ryan had been standing.

Teacup started growling and sniffing furiously. He would have probably followed the scent right to where Ryan was crouched in the bushes if it hadn't been for the sound of the door opening—the human door this time. It opened just a crack at first, and we could hear Mrs. Gutierrez yelling for

Teresa to hurry up or she would be late for ballet.

Now, I guess, Teacup saw his chance to inform the family that Ryan had trespassed. He rushed back toward the house, barking his head off. Only he ran right through the silly string! His tiny legs got tangled up in the plastic-y goo as he ran through the grass.

"Wait!" yelled Ryan, jumping out from behind the bush, but it was too late. The Chihuahua had already pulled the letters out of shape and dragged them across the yard.

Seeing Ryan, Teacup whirled to snap at him and only succeeded in wrapping more of the rubbery string around himself.

Ryan reached toward the tangle then snatched his hands away from Teacup's needle-sharp teeth.

"What do I do?" he said.

The rest of us dudes popped up from behind the hedge...with absolutely no suggestions.

Meanwhile, Teacup dodged Ryan, scrambled up the stairs and hobbled across the porch.

About that time Mrs. Gutierrez and Teresa

came out the front door. Teresa was wearing a coat over her leotard and ballet tights. Both stopped dead in surprise as they saw Teacup swathed in a neon cocoon and stuck halfway through his doggy door.

Ryan knelt on the stairs at their feet looking guilty. "Uh, Hi Teresa!" he said, over the noise of her dog yelping.

Lucky for him, Teresa was dressed for ballet instead of karate—and she was gonna be late. Mrs. Gutierrez didn't waste time being astonished. She just pried Teacup out of the doggy door, tucked him under her arm like a rabid handbag and hustled her daughter around Ryan, down the steps, and into the car.

She didn't spare a glance for the other four Dudes, standing open-mouthed with our heads showing over the tops of the bushes. But, as they drove away, we could hear Teacup baying for blood from behind the closed windows of the minivan.

After that, we figured either Ryan's love was

doomed or his ankles were. Teresa was never going to see him as anything more than a chew-toy for her dog.

Really, the Dudes should have been happy about the way things turned out. Now nothing could come between us and our leader. But it didn't really feel like a win after seeing the look on Ryan's face.

"I've never seen one of his plans completely fail before," moaned Connor. "And now we have to spend the whole weekend with Dad and *his* girl-friend," he added.

Ryan looked pretty grim as they climbed into the cab of Tina's truck. He didn't even trip Connor or wrestle him for the window seat. It seemed like Ryan had lost more than a girlfriend.

But, on Sunday, Ryan came home with a huge heart-shaped box and a familiar grin.

"Dad gave me some advice," said Ryan.

"And Tina gave him the box," put in Connor. Then he added cheerfully, "She let *me* finish the candy!"

The next day, Ryan walked up to Teresa's house with the big heart-shaped box under his arm. He rang the doorbell and Teacup came racing out to gnaw on his leg. Ryan didn't even grimace (mainly because he was wearing his catcher's shin guards from little league under his pants).

When Teresa opened the door, he held out the heart-shaped box. "I know you like surprises, Teresa," Ryan said, "so I brought something for Teacup."

Then, with a flourish, he set the box on the floor and opened it up to reveal two dozen dog treats crammed inside.

With a strangled yelp, Teacup stopped yapping and started eating, snuffling his way forward until he was standing right in the box.

"Oh!" said Teresa. Then she up and kissed him right on the cheek—Ryan, not the dog. (I know because the rest of us were in the bushes making gagging faces.)

Then Ryan and Teresa went inside, and the rest of the Dudes went back to Connor's house to eat junk food and practice dragon kicks.

"So you're okay with Tina now?" I asked Connor.

He shrugged. "Dad said she's not better than mom, just different," Connor explained. Then he summed up the difference this way: "Mom drives a minivan. Tina drives a truck."

I'm guessing the Valentine chocolates didn't hurt Tina's case.

Anyway, Ryan had finally got his girlfriend. Of course, we didn't hear the rest of the story of Ryan and Teresa's love affair until after their break-up—which was about seventeen minutes later.

"I don't care what Dad says. Girls aren't worth it!" Ryan told us when he got home.

This wasn't exactly news to the Dudes. But Connor asked, "What happened?"

So Ryan told us: "It wasn't so bad at first," he said. "Her mom offered me a soda. And Teresa led me to the rec room. I thought we were going to play video games, but it was worse, much worse," he said ominously.

We all sat on the edge of our seats.

"We had no sooner walked in," Ryan said, "than Teresa goes, 'Oh! Sweetie is out!'" (I noticed he gave his Teresa impression a scornful lilt.)

"She dragged me over to one of those aquarium tanks," he said. "You know the one where you can never see anything but a pile of rocks?"

We all nodded. Back in the summer, the Dudes had checked out Teresa's pets a few times when we went over to play video games. She had all kinds—hamsters, lizards...

"That's when I saw it!" said Ryan, his face turning pale. "It was out from under its rock, all right, crouching there on hairy legs, staring at me with all those eyes."

Ryan swallowed and mopped the sweat off his forehead. "That's when I learned the awful truth about Teresa," he said, "the thing that will always keep us apart."

He shuddered as he told us: "She has a pet tarantula!"

Party On! Dudes

Now that his romance with Teresa was over, Ryan's thoughts returned to his first love: the Elephant Gun. We'd done pretty well on the Sushirasers we'd bought with my birthday money and Nate's robot money (too bad Deven had already spent all his money on hair). Most of the girls were working on their Bento collections and were eager to purchase.

Nate told us we had accumulated almost 30,000 Bucks. "If we can sell another crate of Sushirasers," he said, "I'd say we will have enough Bucks to safely outbid anyone for the Elephant Gun at auction."

"We have to *buy* another crate before we can sell one," Connor pointed out. "And we're out of money—real money, I mean."

A solution came the next week at dinner

time—not that we were eating. Mom wasn't home yet, and Dad was still cooking.

"I'm hungry," announced Jayden for like the twelfth time.

Dad sighed and stirred the pot. "Dinner's almost ready," he said for probably the thirteenth time.

I was doing my homework at the kitchen table, where I could keep an eye out in case food ever became available.

Leon was sitting in his high chair. He gets to eat early, but he only eats mush. It's good-for-you organic mush that mom makes on the weekend and freezes in ice cube trays. Dad is supposed to heat it up, but he figured out that Leon likes the frozen cubes. Dad's smart with shortcuts like that—except when he's cooking. So Leon was eating a mush-sicle, and he was still better off than Jayden and me.

Then Mom came home.

"Hi, Mom!" I said.

"Dinner's not ready yet," Jayden informed her.

After she kissed our heads and hung her purse on the chair, she said to Dad, "Do you need any help?"

Dad smiled thinly. "No thanks. I'm just a little off schedule," he explained. "Mrs. Kostenko stopped me in the driveway and gave me a casserole."

"Oh dear," Mom said. "She must have noticed you're at home and thinks you're out of work."

"I'm *not* out of work," Dad grumbled. "I just don't have a client yet." He sprinkled something and peered into the pot.

I peered at fractions.

Jayden peered at Leon.

Leon rubbed mush across his cheeks.

"Well, if you need help, just say so," said Mom, scooping a gob of mush out of Leon's ear.

Dad looked up with his glasses all steamed and said, "I've got it all under control."

"What did you do with the casserole?" Jayden asked hopefully, which was a sure sign of his desperation for food—even food that had been horrifically comingled and adulterated with flavorings.

"I put the casserole in the freezer for safe-keeping," said Dad stirring harder. "I don't need any help putting supper on the table."

"Of course you don't," Mom soothed.

Meanwhile, Jayden had remembered some-thing else that was in the freezer for safekeeping.

"Mom! Can I have my snowball?" he asked, jumping up and down. I guess he forgot he had saved it for Leon. But then, Leon already had frozen mush.

"It's still there isn't it?" Jayden asked, stretching his neck to try to see in the freezer when she opened the door.

"Of course it is," she assured him. "Safe and sound."

Mom used a fork to chip Jay's snowball off of where it had stuck to a bag of frozen peas. Then she handed it to him in a bowl.

"Cool!" said Jayden, marveling at a snowball in April. I figured he was gonna eat it.

Dad stirred the sauce harder. "Just because we're both working and have a new baby doesn't mean we're not on top of things," he said.

"Right," said Mom. "And you'll probably get a client any day."

"Right," said Dad.

"Mom?" said Jayden.

"Jayden, please don't interrupt the conversation," Mom replied. She frowned absently at his empty snowball bowl.

"We'll know when we need to ask for help," Dad said.

"Of course," Mom agreed.

"And that time hasn't come," said Dad.

"Right," said Mom.

Dad was staring at the sauce recipe on his phone when it suddenly rang, causing him to jerk and nearly drop it in the pot.

"Hello?" Dad said. Then his eyes widened. He dropped the spoon in the sauce, stuck his finger in his other ear, and dashed out of the room.

"Mom?" said Jayden.

"Please wait, Jayden," she said, nervously glancing toward the room where Dad went.

In a minute, Dad came back with a weird

look on his face. "I got a client!" he said in amazement.

"Wonderful!" said Mom, and I came out of my hunger coma to cheer.

Dad told us all about it. "That was the systems administrator over at...blah, blah, blah" (well, I didn't actually pay attention to what he said.)

Anyway, in a minute, Mom said, "Are you sure you can do all that and take care of the kids? Maybe you should call your father."

"I don't need help." Dad said it cheerfully now. He dumped the sauce over spaghetti in a bowl, forgetting that Jayden likes his noodles plain.

I happily tossed my math worksheet over my shoulder to make room for a dinner plate.

Jayden said, "Mom?"

Mom smiled down at the little guy at last. "Yes, Jayden," she said pleasantly. "Thank you for being so patient. What did you want to talk about?"

"I want to talk about my birthday!"

I looked up to see Dad freeze and Mom sink down into one of the kitchen chairs. She glanced at the calendar.

"Jayden's birthday is next weekend!" Mom said in her fake happy tone—the one she uses for talking to PTA members who want her to do something.

"Of course," said Dad. "It happens every year at this time," he pointed out intelligently.

Jayden nodded.

Last year we had the party at the bouncy house because that's where you go when you have to invite the whole preschool and the kids are too young for the trampoline place.

Mom's eyes widened. "It's too late to book the bouncy house," she realized.

"It's too expensive anyway," said Dad. "And we don't want to invite the whole kindergarten."

Mom turned to Jayden. "We want to invite your *closest* friends, Jayden. And we'll do something special here."

Dad checked the weather report on his phone. "It's supposed to be clear, so we can have the party in the yard. That'll save cleaning up the house." (Another good short-cut. Dad's always thinking!)

Mom was thinking too: "We'll need decorations and plates and cups—I can get those after work. You'll have to organize some games," she told Dad.

She turned to Jayden, her confidence returning. "The party can be about anything you want, sweetheart—superheroes or firemen or trains..."

"Dudes," said Jayden.

"Dudes?" she asked.

"Dudes," Jayden repeated firmly.

Mom and Dad looked at each other.

Then Dad said, "I think we need help."

"Can't blame the little dude for thinking we're awesome," said Ryan when he showed up the next day.

He was right. We were celebrities to the kindergarteners. It wasn't just because of all the stuff Listening Bear "wrote" after spending winter break at our house. Apparently, Jayden had given out the URL for our zombie video and it had gone viral with the five- and six-year-old set.

Of course, they don't print plates with our faces on them. Yet. That's why Mom and Dad had invited the Dudes over for a planning session to get tips on how to create a Dudes-themed birthday party. (You might want to listen for pointers too!)

Mom had us all sit at the kitchen table. She even had a pad of paper ready to write down ideas.

"Let's call it Dudes-o-rama!" suggested Deven, "No! Dudes-a-palooza!"

Mom wrote: Jayden's 6th Birthday Party.

She looked up at the Dudes. "What kind of snacks would be Dude food?" she asked.

"Powdered donuts," said Connor.

"Cheesy puffs," chimed in Nate.

Then Ryan snapped his fingers. "At my uncle's wedding they had this fountain that sprayed chocolate!" he said.

Mom shuddered. She wrote: Grapes and cheese chunks.

"And, of course, I'll make a birthday cake," she added. She wrote down: cake and ice cream.

"Now, we'll need some nice games to keep the children occupied," she said, looking around the table. "Something like musical chairs?"

Connor grinned. "Only we could use cool music," he suggested, "like 'Rock Down the Walls'."

"DUUUUUDES!" hooted Deven, making Mom and Dad jump and Leon start squealing over the monitor.

"I'll get the baby," said Mom to Dad as she fled the room. "You stay here and talk to Tyler's friends."

When she was gone, Dad leaned forward. "Look, boys," he whispered, "Meg will send email invitations, and she'll buy the supplies. But I'm going to be really busy over the next week. How about I hire you to plan the party?"

The Dudes looked at each other. We could use the money to buy more Sushirasers!

Ryan and Dad shook hands on the deal right away. Then Ryan shook hands with me and Nate and Deven and Connor. Then we each shook hands with Dad and with each other.

We were still doing that when Mom came

back carrying Leon. "I see you got things settled," she said hopefully.

"Don't worry about a thing, Mrs. Reynolds," said Ryan. "It's going to be epic."

"Dudes is a great theme," added Nate.

"We can teach the little guys how to be just like us!" said Deven.

Mom looked uncertainly at Dad, but he shrugged it off.

Then Ryan smiled his car-salesman grin at Leon and gave him a tiny high five. "It'll be your turn in no time, baby dude!" he said.

On Wednesday night, Mom bought the "Boys Birthday Kit" from the warehouse store.

The Dudes met in my basement after school on Thursday to plan the party.

"A kid's party is three hours," said Nate. "I estimate that cake and ice cream will take up fifteen minutes of that time and opening presents will take another fifteen minutes. That leaves two and a half hours to fill with Dudes-related activities."

We opened up the big box. Inside were streamers, balloons, party hats, cups, plates, napkins, paper tablecloths and goodie bags, all in bright colors.

Ryan gave a thumbs-up. "We can use all this stuff," he said.

There were also star stickers and a piñata shaped like a comically small dinosaur with a long neck and googly eyes.

"Aw! Look at the baby-saurus," said Deven.

"That's an Apatosaurus," Nate corrected.

Deven patted it on the head. "I call him Donald," he said. Then he waved the dino in Nate's face.

"Rawr!" growled Deven.

Nate was unperturbed. "The Apatosaurus was herbivorous," he pointed out.

"I hope that means he ate a lot of candy," said Deven shaking the piñata to hear it rattle.

"How's a dinosaur going to fit with our theme?" Connor asked.

"What did you expect," snapped Ryan, "a piñata of Sensei's face?"

"How about yours?" returned Connor, making it clear he was ready to bust something.

"Stick to the point, guys," I said, before they could get started whaling on each other. "We've got a party to plan."

"Speaking of points," said Deven, "what do we do with these?"

When I looked, he was wearing five cone-shaped party hats. The points stuck out all over his head, making him look like a new kind of Pokemon.

Ryan ignored Deven. "Tyler's right, Dudes," he said. "We're getting paid for this. If we do a good job, it could be a whole new career."

"If Jayden has fun," I pointed out. After all, it was my little brother's birthday we were testing this on.

"We'll give the little dude a good time," said Ryan.

"The kindergarteners worship the ground we walk on," said Nate.

And Connor just had to add, "What could go wrong?"

Dudes-a-palooza

"It's J-Day, Dudes," Ryan said on the day of the party. "Time for Operation Ballistic Bash!"

The Dudes filled some balloons with helium and a bunch more with water and waited for the kids to arrive.

Jayden had invited four of his best friends. *At least we won't be outnumbered*, I thought, remembering that the kindergarteners had been learning karate in P.E. too. But there were actually six guests:

Jayden, Cello, Alex C., Alex H., Alex R. and Listening Bear. Yeah, that's right. We had a bear wearing a sweater as one of the guests at our party.

Alex C. brought him (it was his weekend), and the others shouted, "Hi, L.B.!" and ran over as soon as they saw him. What can I say? The kindergarteners love the bear.

Alex R. even gave L.B. a big hug. (Alex R. was a girl, by the way.) She knew what Jayden liked, though. They all did. We opened presents first, and he got a dart gun, a cap gun, a water gun, and a marshmallow gun. (The bear didn't get him anything.)

Since Jayden liked shooting so much, we had decided to go with a military theme for the activities. First we had all the kids paint their faces with camouflage. That was pretty easy. I mean, you just give them green and brown face paint and no instructions and it comes out camo!

It was going well until I accidentally called Cello "Jello" and he head-butted my stomach. I ended up with his face-print on my shirt.

Time for Deven's drill sergeant routine. He started by inhaling a little helium to make his voice high and squeaky. Then he lined up the kids and shouted orders at them, all the while sounding like some crazed cartoon character.

"Today, we are going to teach you how to be Dudes," he cheeped. *"First, you must learn the battle cry. DUUUUUDE!"*

"DUUUUUDE!" hooted the kindergarteners.

"Now do a chicken dance!" he peeped.

The kids started flapping their arms and clucking.

"Put on your party hats!" Deven squealed commandingly.

The kids put on their sharp, pointy hats. Then Cello lowered his head and made ready to charge!

*"Take **off** your hats!"* Deven hastily screeched as I grabbed the little rhino and re-moved his horn. (What *was* it with this kid and head-butting?)

"Looks like the little dudes came ready for action," Connor remarked.

"I believe we need to dissipate some of their energy," said Nate.

"Time for Wheels of War!" Ryan announced.

Wheels of War was one of the Dudes' favor-ite games. Each kid got a dart gun and a vehicle: we had trikes and big wheels and scooters ready in the driveway. (Listening Bear rode in the basket on Jayden's trike.) Each kid also got a cardboard shield and a goodie-bag full of ammo. Then we blocked off the cul-de-sac and let them at it!

The goal of Wheels of War is to drive around and shoot at the other drivers. Of course, the other drivers are all shooting at you too, so you better block with your shield. But here's where we'd jazzed it up for the party: If a dart hit you, one of the Dudes would come over and stick a star sticker to the spot with about a foot of red streamer attached. As the kids raced around, the streamers blew out behind to look like blood streaming from the wound. And if you got wounded three times, you were out. Little kids love these realistic games.

When there was one kindergartener left, we called a stop. The winner had only one streamer hanging off his ear. Technically, that was a headshot, but I didn't count it as an instant kill. Kids this age weren't up to understanding the finer nuances of the game. I looked into the short kid's mottled green face and said, "Way to go, uh, Alex!" (That seemed like a safe guess.) He turned out to be C.

Nate checked his watch. That game had taken about a minute and a half, and the Dudes were already panting from running around sticking on wounds. I realized it was going to be a long haul to the cake.

"For our next activity," yelled Ryan as cheerfully as our music teacher, Ms Larkey. "We're going to teach you to smash through a window!" Then he added, "My brother, Connor, will demonstrate!"

"DUUUUUDE!" hooted the kids, jumping up and down.

"Destruction appears to be very popular," Nate noted.

Ryan held up one of the empty screen frames my granddad had built for the shed. He hadn't put the screen in yet, so the window was just a square-shaped hoop.

Then Connor ran down the yard and threw himself through it. He dived through, actually, did a summersault in the grass, and rolled to his feet. Meanwhile, Ryan waved his hands toward Connor like he was showing off a prize-winning pig.

"Ooooh," said the kids appreciatively.

Next we brought out the other frames we'd

borrowed from Granddad. To these we had taped
the paper tablecloths that came in the Birthday Kit.
So each kid got to crash through a colored "window". Cool huh?

Jayden and his friends loved it—even the
ones who landed on their heads. When they were
finished, they looked around eagerly for other
obstacles to smash. That's when Ryan announced
we'd be going inside.

In the basement, the kids dressed up in our
old Halloween costumes: knight's armor, SWAT
team vests, army helmets, etc. Even Listening Bear
got into the act with a ninja mask and sash made
out of old scarves.

Then each little dude got a chance to try
Instant Obliteration: Survival Mode. (It was lucky
we'd already built a great game to use for the party.) None of the kindergarteners managed to rescue Sensei. But the look of maniacal glee on their
little green faces as they smashed down the walls
and whacked things with foam swords couldn't
help but warm your heart.

I was beginning to feel pretty good about

this party. Jayden and his friends were having a great time, and the Dudes were totally in control.

That's when Ryan yelled, "Target practice! Everybody outside!"

As we herded the kids out the basement's sliding door, I could see that Dad had set up card tables in the backyard, and Mom was bringing out the plates, cups, and plastic utensils. It must be getting close to cake time.

Meanwhile, we led the kids into the side yard, which the Dudes had turned into a shoot-ing gallery. Deven had drawn angry faces on the helium balloons, and Nate had tied them along the hedge so the little dudes could shoot at them with dart guns. (We had thought of attaching needles to the darts so the balloons would actually pop, but then Ryan pointed out that would be irresponsible: It might screw up the dart guns or something.)

Ryan shouted "Commence firing!"

A hail of darts flew over the hedge, totally missing their targets. Of course, their aim might have been spoiled by the costume sleeves bunched up around their arms or the helmets falling down over their eyes. Besides that, the balloons swayed a little in the breeze, making them moving targets. Anyway, the kids kept missing, and those angry balloon faces kept bobbing up and down, mocking the shooters, until one of the Alexes finally snapped.

He dashed to the cake table, grabbed a plastic fork, and made an insane bayonet charge on the balloon! Following his lead, the other kids dropped their dart guns and took up the forks of vengeance too!

Naturally, the Dudes retreated. After all, it wasn't our fight.

"You got the flags ready?" Ryan asked calmly over the sound of frenzied war cries and popping balloons.

"Right here," said Connor, pulling two bandannas out of his pocket.

When the Dudes returned to the side yard the balloon massacre was over. Ryan paced in front of the hedge, inspecting the troops like he was General Patton or something.

"Listen up wanna-be Dudes," he said.

The kindergarteners turned their big eyes on our leader.

"You have done well on the training exercises," said Ryan. "Now it's time to prove that you are real Dudes."

The little Dudes stood up straighter. And Jayden held up Listening Bear.

"You're now going up against us Dudes in a war game called Capture the Flag," Ryan said, trying not to lock eyes with the bear. He held up the bandannas. (Connor had used a permanent marker to draw a J on one and a D on the other.)

"The mission is to get the other team's flag," Ryan explained, "either by stealth or by attack."

"But no forks!" put in Deven worriedly. "There are no forks in this game."

Ryan nodded. "Each team has a leader," he said, handing the J flag to Jayden. "Now go choose a place to hang your flag!"

Jayden clutched Listening Bear and the bandanna to his chest and led the little kids toward the basement door.

Meanwhile, the Dudes displayed our flag

on the treehouse. There was no point in hiding it, since we were gonna let the little guys win eventually. Of course, we might as well repel a few assaults first, to keep it interesting.

We figured any minute the kindergarteners would come running out to attack us. But they didn't. We sat around the treehouse, watching Mom pour red punch into the paper cups on the card table.

"It's quiet," said Deven, "*too* quiet."

"I wish my spy robot was finished so we could send it to see what they are doing," Nate remarked.

"Maybe they're waiting for *us* to attack *them*," said Connor.

"Yeah," said Ryan, climbing down from the treehouse. The five of us trooped across the yard and surrounded the basement door.

"On my mark..." said Ryan, "GO!"

Nate opened the sliding glass door, and the Dudes burst into the room.

The kids were all sitting in the floor playing with Jayden's Matchbox cars. They didn't even look up.

"We're here to capture your flag!" warned Ryan menacingly.

"You can't," said Jayden.

"We already won," said Cello.

I rolled my eyes.

Ryan chuckled. "You're supposed to try to get *our* flag," he explained.

"We got your leader instead," said Alex R. "That's better."

Leave it to kindergarteners to play the game wrong, I thought. Maybe we should have ended the game right then. Maybe we would have if Deven hadn't suddenly gasped.

"Guys, look!" He pointed toward the television set. On the shelf above it sat the cat carrier, open and empty.

"They kidnapped our sensei!" cried Deven.

We all whirled to face the kindergarteners.

"Why did you do that?" asked Connor.

"Sensei's not our leader!" spluttered Ryan.

"Where's Sensei, Jayden?" I demanded.

"Somewhere safe," he answered cryptically.

"I know how to find out," said Ryan. "All we have to do is capture *their* leader."

He reached for Jayden, but, at that moment, all the little kids dropped their cars and ran screaming in different directions.

The Dudes looked at Ryan.

"Well," he said, "we can't let ourselves get beat by a bunch of kindergarteners. Catch those little dudes!"

It was tougher than you'd think. I pulled an army helmet off one kid only to see Alex R.'s braids fall over her shoulders.

Connor was gaining on another Alex, but, as he lunged, he tripped over the kid's cape and rolled head over heels as the green-faced little hero dashed away.

"Get the backpack!" yelled Nate.

Sure enough, Cello was wearing Jayden's school backpack. Inside the pack, a suspicious gnome-sized bundle bounced against his back.

Ryan and I finally cornered him and unzipped the backpack only to find Listening Bear inside. The Dudes had gathered around by then, and the little dudes joined us.

"They got our leader!" wailed Cello.

"What? *Jayden's* your leader," I said.

Jayden shook his head. "We voted," he said. "Besides, the flag had an 'L' for Listening Bear."

"That was a 'J'," I argued, even as I remembered that Jayden still prints 'J' backwards half the time. He gets confused on 'L' and 'b' and 'd' too.

Meanwhile, the other Dudes stood there in silence, absorbing the idea that the Kindergarteners had elected a teddy bear to lead them—and they were winning.

Suddenly, Deven grabbed Listening Bear and shook him. "Tell us where Sensei is!" he shrieked.

Connor took the bear before Deven could start putting bamboo under its fingernails.

At least Nate had a sensible plan. "We need time to search for Sensei," he whispered. "I suggest we distract the enemy with a diversion."

"I know just the thing," I said.

I turned to Ryan with a salute. "Permission to deploy Private Donald, Sir?"

Ryan grinned. "Permission granted," he said. "It's time for Operation Dude-a-Saurus!"

Okay, imagine, if you will, the usual party scene when the piñata comes out:

You blindfold a little kid and give him a big stick. He starts whaling away at the colorful crea-ture, intent on destruction. Small children hover close by, watching for a successful blow, ready to swoop in under the flailing club and grab up a handful of cheap candy.

I know you see the problem here: Only *one* child gets to take part in the festive slaying of the beast!

Now, the Dudes are generally in favor of whacking things with big sticks. But, for Jayden's party, we had come up with a more inclusive way to defeat old Donald the Dinosaur.

First, we gathered the little dudes and marched them up the deck stairs where they could stand at the rail, looking down at Nate.

Nate pointed to the piñata in the grass be-side him.

"This menacing creature has arrived from

space," he announced. (He'd gotten the idea from an old science fiction movie.)

Alex C. raised his hand. "That's a dinosaur," he said.

Nate nodded approvingly. "It is an Apato-saurus," he said.

"Dinosaurs are extinct," said Alex H.

"Not in space," Nate replied reasonably.

"How did it breathe in space?" asked Alex R.

"It had a space ship," said Nate.

"A dinosaur wouldn't fit in a space ship," challenged Cello.

"This is a small dinosaur," Nate pointed out.

"What happened to his ship?" Jayden asked.

"It was vaporized in the atmosphere," Nate explained.

I had to admire him for having so many quick answers, but this could go on all day. Luckily, Ryan interrupted. "The point is that you need to defend the Earth by bombing the dinosaur," he said, "*with these.*"

He gestured to where Connor and I were lugging a laundry basket out onto the deck. Suddenly there were no more questions. The basket was full of 100 water balloons.

"DUUUUUDE!" hooted the little dudes, pouncing on the basket.

During the bombardment, the big Dudes searched the yard, the basement, and the house. But there was no sign of Sensei anywhere. I was beginning to wish he really did have the power of telepathy like on **Ninja Tempest** so he could send us a mental message about where he was hidden.

Meanwhile, I guess we gave the little guys too long to defeat the dinosaur. By the time we got back, they had finished off the water balloons and started using a bomb of their own design—party hats filled with fruit punch off the party table. (You had to admire their creativity.)

I saw Jayden drop his bomb for a direct hit that punctured Donald's back and splatted on the now-sodden lump of candy in his stomach.

"The red part's nuclear," Cello explained.

"I knew those pointy hats were dangerous!" said Deven.

I peeked over the rail at ground zero. What

I saw was grisly. Donald's long neck drooped.
His tail had separated from his body. The whole
scene appeared to be splashed with blood. And, of
course, he was radioactive.

That's when we heard: "Happy Birthday to
you!"

Mom's voice warbled brightly as she came
through the sliding door carrying a tray. The little
kids all dropped their last shells and joined her,
singing as they followed her down the steps like
little angels and took their places around the table.
Jayden sat at the head, surrounded by four children
and one bear.

"Who gets the bear's cake?" Connor whispered.

"Never mind that," Deven whispered back.
"Where's Sensei?"

Nate shrugged. "We've searched every-
where," he said.

The kids had used a lot of energy on their
bombardment and were getting thirsty.

"I thought I filled those cups," said Mom in
confusion.

"I'll get more drinks," Dad offered. He ran back toward the deck stairs, veering around Donald's devastated corpse. Meanwhile, Mom set the cake in front of Jayden.

"Their moms will be coming soon," I hissed to the guys.

"We've got to get Sensei back before the little dudes start leaving," said Ryan.

"Quiet!" warned Deven. He eyed L.B. and whispered, "The bear is listening!"

"Oh dear! I forgot the ice cream," said Mom, and she too, ran back up the deck stairs to the kitchen.

When she was gone I pleaded, "Come on, Jay. Tell us where Sensei is!"

Jayden grinned, causing his camo to crack and drop green and brown flecks on his plate. "He's in a safe place," he said.

I was beginning to panic. Through the side yard, I could see an SUV pulling up to the curb out front. The parents were coming. We were out of time.

Then Ryan said "Look!"

We all looked where he was pointing.

Mom was carrying her tray down the deck stairs. On it was a tub of ice cream, a scoop...and a plaster garden gnome.

"DUUUUUDE!" shouted Deven in greeting.

"DUUUUUDE!" echoed the little kids.

"Look what I found in the freezer," Mom said, giving me a confused look as five kindergarteners (and Deven) offered respectful ninja bows in the gnome's direction.

I took Sensei from her and set him in the middle of the table. "That's our centerpiece," I explained quickly, ignoring the way Deven was rubbing the gnome to warm its hands and feet.

Mom shook her head.

Jayden blew out the candles.

Dad handed out juice boxes.

And the parents arrived just in time to make small talk and watch their little ones eat cake with their hands.

Alex C's mother looked from the face-print on my shirt, to the garden gnome wearing a party hat to the scary balloon face deflated on the hedge.

"I'm not sure I understand your theme," she said.

"Uh, it was sort of action/adventure," said Dad hastily, before Deven could hoot again.

Ryan sauntered over to Alex H.'s dad, who was staring down at the puddle of fruit punch and melted piñata. "We might be available to do this at *your* home," he hinted.

Last thing, Connor handed out empty good-ie bags. The parents were puzzled, but the kids beamed like they'd always wanted something to hold their extra ammo.

"Thank you. I had a good time!" called little Alex R. politely from the car. Then I heard her tell her mother, "We used nuclear bombs, and I got wounded three times!"

Talk about your good word-of-mouth! (It was probably my imagination that her mother gunned the engine as she pulled her minivan away from the curb.)

By the way, he didn't say much, but I'm pret-ty sure Listening Bear had a good time too. And, of course, Sensei looked great in all the pictures!

Dude-o-nomics

With the success of Jayden's party, the dudes were flush with cash. We bought more Sushirasers, and they sold like crazy.

Speaking of crazy: When Melanie bought a Sushiraser before school and Kiley fell out of her seat in class trying to see which one, Mr. Isaak just rolled his eyes. But, when he caught Sathya and Melanie whispering during a test--and then found out they weren't cheating but arranging to trade two Firefly Squid for one Tako Taco--he had no choice but to confiscate their Sushirasers.

Of course, to the Dudes, that meant both girls would be in the market for more.

Then, in Mrs. Hancock's room, Emma got distracted by the Wasabi Flower on Sophie's desk and forgot to hand out worksheets to half the class. Mrs. Hancock took the Sushiraser, which meant

Sophie needed another Wasabi Flower, and now Emma wanted one too.

The Dudes were laughing all the way to the Coconut bank...

...until Ms Finch let Kimiko call her mother because she'd forgotten her Bento Box (and it turned out she didn't mean her *lunch*box).

I guess that was the last straw.

The fifth-grade teachers had a meeting.

The next morning, it was not Deven's cheerful tones but Mr Isaak's voice of doom we heard when the intercom squawked:

```
The fifth-grade teachers wish to announce
that, due to many recent cases of flagrant
disregard for the rules, the fifth-grade field
trip will now require a fee of 1000 Coconut
Bucks.

Any student who has not accrued that amount
through good behavior will be left out of
the field trip and spend the time doing brain
games in the library.
```

Before he clicked off, I could hear Deven's

voice in the background, squalling, "Not brain games! Agggh!"

But it was no joke.

"How do you like the teachers playing such a dirty trick?" Ryan complained as we gathered on the Dude-hammock for recess.

He gripped the cargo net with white knuckles. "Just when we've nearly got enough money for the Elephant Gun!" he grumbled. "Now we'll have to spend 5000 Bucks on the field trip."

"We may be the only ones," said Nate ominously.

"Huh?" said Deven.

Nate began to explain. "By my calculations, there are approximately $45,000 Bucks in circulation," he said.

"But they're *not* in circulation," I pointed out. "The Dudes have most of them."

"Exactly," Nate agreed. "If *we* are holding most of the currency, our classmates cannot have enough Bucks to go on the field trip."

"This is bad," said Connor, hanging upside down. "Girls will start saving for the trip, and stop spending their Bucks with us."

But Nate shook his head. "It's worse than you think," he explained. "If our classmates can't raise 1000 Bucks in time, there won't *be* a class trip."

Apparently, it doesn't pay to be the only five rich kids in the school.

"What can we do about it?" Connor asked. "We can't give back the Bucks we've got."

"No," said Ryan, absently flicking shredded rubber at Connor's face. "We need more Bucks in circulation."

Nate turned to him suddenly. "You're saying we need to stimulate inflation!" he said.

"Huh?" said Deven.

Nate put his brain (and his mouth) in high gear. "Inflation is a rapid increase in the money required to operate an economy," he explained. "In response to certain crises a government can sometimes be persuaded to print more currency."

"What kind of crisis?" I asked.

Nate answered, "Usually war or depression."

"I'll be depressed if we don't go on a field

trip!" Deven proclaimed.

"The teachers aren't a government," I pointed out.

"But they do print the Bucks," Nate said. "The template is on the staff server so each teacher can print as many as she needs to distribute to her students."

"Then all we need to do is convince a teacher to print more Bucks," Ryan mused. He leaned back and put his hands behind his head to think.

"We need a thousand Bucks for every fifth grader," said Connor.

"And there's only a month left until the field trip," I pointed out. "That's a lot of good behavior in a short time."

"We'll need a very positive teacher..." mused Nate.

"Or a crazy one," I added.

"Right on both counts," said Ryan with a smile.

The music teacher, Ms Larkey, was the most

positive teacher we had at Sherwood School. Her class sucked. Between the goofy songs she made us sing and that way she had of flapping her hands when we weren't singing—like she was directing the music of life—it was a pretty tough hour to get through.

Ms Larkey was also the kind of person who liked to "give old melodies a happy makeover" by replacing the original words with new ones.

That's why, for the Veteran's Day assembly, we sang "You're a Grand Old Seal" and "I'm a Sherwood Doodle Dandy!" (Thus making visiting veterans wish they were back in the war.)

On this particular day, Ms Larkey had us doing an "Exploration of Percussion", which wasn't bad because at least we got to use instruments like the triangle and the glockenspiel and the bongos and the guiro.

"Ooh! Me! I want the weirdo!" shouted Deven, throwing his hand up.

Ms Larkey smiled graciously, dancing toward him with mincing steps. "You pronounce it 'wee-roh'," she said, handing Deven the instrument.

"Weirdo!" repeated Deven.

"Wee-roh!" said Ms Larkey musically.

"Weir-doh!" sang Deven, his voice cracking on the high note.

"Wiro, wiro, wiro," she sang like a jungle bird.

"Weirdo, weirdo, weirdo!" returned Deven his voice screeching and his head bobbing to the beat.

"What wonderful rhythm Deven has!" said Ms Larkey joyously. "Class, let's all copy Deven's rhythm," she said.

"Weirdo-weirdo-weirdo," said the class, not quite so joyously.

Ms Larkey clasped her hands. "Now, who knows what type of notes we were just singing?" she asked.

The fifth graders remained silent.

"Nobody? Well then it must be time to re-view the rhythm song!"

The class groaned.

Ms Larkey skipped to the piano with glee. She had made up the Rhythm Song to the tune of

"Twinkle, Twinkle Little Star":

> *When you play or sing at school,*
> *Rhythm is the golden rule.*
> *Measure time and do not cheat.*
> *Quarter notes get just one beat...*

The song had eight verses describing each kind of note and how many beats it got. And every kid in school had to memorize it.

Ms Larkey was very proud of how educational the Rhythm Song was. She even put an MP3 of herself singing it on the school website so anybody who wanted to could learn it and, I don't know, sing it in the shower or something.

We had to do it every week in her class (sing the Rhythm Song, not take a shower.) It seemed to last forever. Unlike Ms Larkey, the kids didn't put much heart into it, and the sound kind of got slower and sadder as the song progressed until we finally ground to a halt with:

> *Know each note before you play.*

Sing it in the rhythmic way!

Ms Larkey didn't seem to notice the dying moose quality. "That was *lovely*, students," she said. "You have such *beautiful* voices."

See what I mean? Ms Larkey was the perfect positive pushover for Operation Inflation.

"I have the sign-up sheets for the Sherwood School Talent Show which is coming up next month," Ms Larkey told us. "Now who is planning on entering?"

Nobody raised their hand except Teresa.

Ms Larkey shook her head. "I know you are all talented," she insisted.

That's when Ryan raised his hand. "We're not professionals, Ms Larkey," he said. "I mean, it's not like anyone would *pay* us to sing."

"Yeah!" hinted Deven. "We wouldn't be so shy if we earned BIG BUCKS!"

Ms Larkey shimmied with excitement. "I have an electrifying idea, my darlings!" she said. "I'm going to offer 500 Coconut Bucks to each person who performs in the talent show."

That made the class sit up and take notice. I was just glad the Dudes had all the Bucks we needed.

"The Talent Show is lame," Ryan confirmed in a whisper as he watched the other kids crowding to sign up.

Ms Larkey fluttered over to the piano. "Now I know that many students decide to lip-synch to a professionally recorded tune, but you all have such *sweet* voices. Let's hear them now," she said, striking up the Rhythm Song again.

The class gave a whole note groan.

Ms Larkey solved our problem of increasing the supply of currency. It wasn't just the talent show. For the next month, she handed out Bucks as fast as she could print them:

She rewarded girls in the lunchroom for screeching along with Troy Diamond.

When Mitch Dugal broke his ankle and had to use crutches, Ms Larkey rewarded him for walking down the hall with a syncopated rhythm.

She rewarded Janelle Veitch just for *listening* to music (right before Ms Grieber confiscated her MP3 player).

She even tried to pay a little kid for dancing when he was actually just in a hurry to get to the bathroom!

Ms Larkey's printer was really humming— which was just what we needed if we wanted to save the fifth-grade field trip.

It was a lucky thing the Dudes were set for Bucks. We were just about the only fifth-graders who *didn't* have to perform in the Talent Show. Of course, knowing Ms Larkey, maybe we should have guessed that she might go overboard.

Dudes Got Talent

Good morning Sherwood Students.

The Talent Show is coming up next week. Get your show on to show off!

Today's music in the lunchroom is: Troy Diamond's "Searching for Lunch"—I mean "Love"! Nobody's searching for lunch in there if they're smart.

Today's wisdom is…uh…um…It looks like Ms Larkey has an announcement—either that, or she's doing the chicken dance.

We all winced as Ms Larkey's voice warbled out of the speakers:

Listen up, darlings! With so many entries, this year's Talent Show will be the best Sherwood School has ever had!

And I'm announcing one more sensational piece of news: This year I'm offering a prize to the winning performer or performing group of 25,000 Coconut Bucks!

"This changes our situation," said Nate when we gathered after school.

"But I thought we had plenty of Bucks," Ryan said.

"That's true. Even after paying for each of us to attend the field trip, we still have over twenty-five thousand Bucks among the five of us," Nate explained.

"We're rich!" Deven rejoiced.

But Connor could see the danger. "Wait," he said, calculating fast. "Whoever wins the Talent Show will have almost as much as we do."

Nate nodded. "And if they should have the idea to combine their Bucks with those of others…"

"They could outbid us!" I said.

"Dudes, there's only one thing we can do," said Ryan, and I had a sinking feeling I knew what it was. "We have to enter the Talent Show," he said. "And we have to win!"

Unfortunately, Nate was the only one of us

who could play an instrument—the oboe. Unless you counted the way Deven plays piano—which we didn't. I was seriously worried about looking like a fool on stage. But Ryan said we just needed the right angle.

"I'll make up a song for us!" Deven volunteered. "Once there was a little dude..." he began, which told us three things:

1. It's way too easy to make up a song to the tune of Twinkle, Twinkle Little Star.

2. There are way too many words that rhyme with dude—like lewd, rude, crude, un-glued...And, most importantly:

3. We'd be better off lip-synching than letting Deven sing!

"What's lip-synching?" asked Connor, pursing his mouth like a baboon to try to get a look at his lips.

"You know," Ryan explained, "when you just *pretend* you're singing."

"The idea is to *synch*ronize your lips with a song playing on the speakers," said Nate.

"That sounds easy," said Connor.

"Too easy," I said. "How do we win?"

"The contest is really about popularity, not talent," said Ryan. "At the end, Ms Grieber asks for applause for each group. And the one with the loudest cheers wins."

"Then we need music everybody likes," I said.

Ryan smiled. "I know just the song."

"Rock Down the Walls" by Random Noise was currently the Dudes' favorite song. And the group did this epic video online. It starts with a lone warrior doing a battle cry—kind of a loud HOOOOOT!

In the vid, there's a prison, and the singing group is in chains and everything is shades of gray except the colors in their shaggy hair. All the guards have their heads shaved and tattoos on their foreheads. The prison is a maze with no way out. And there is a monster waiting to devour the hapless band.

Then the chorus starts, and the rockers fight

back. They end up smashing down the maze with their tennis shoes and their strong voices and stuff. The walls fall on the monster and the guards! It's totally awesome. Adults hate it.

Who knows what it was supposed to mean—guys with colorful hair can save the world? Don't let the bald guys get you down? Tennis shoes are stronger than bricks?

"Actually, I believe that the shoes were provided to them by the shoe company as a form of advertisement," Nate explained.

That figures. There's no way down-on-their-luck rockers could afford that brand. Anyway, "Rock Down the Walls" was the perfect song to do in the talent show.

"And we're going to do something way cooler than singing it," Ryan explained. "We're going to act out the video!" He wanted to choreograph the fight scene—that means plan it out, not just whale on each other like he and Connor usually do.

The number one thing we needed was walls. So Nate brought his speakers to my house and put the song on repeat so we could rehearse with the cardboard bricks.

We must have gotten carried away with the time, because, suddenly Mom came rushing down the basement stairs. She was waving her hands and yelling something, but I couldn't hear what.

Nate stopped the music.

"Hi, Mom," called Jayden. "Do you like Random Noise?"

Mom's eyes kind of crossed. "I could hear it from out in the driveway when I got home from work!" she said, as if that were a bad thing.

I wondered if Dad could hear it in the shed. He hadn't said anything.

"What on earth are you doing?" Mom demanded.

Ryan spoke up. "We're practicing our talent, Mrs. Reynolds," he said.

That might have come across better if he and Connor hadn't been wearing post-it notes on their foreheads. (See, Nate was trying out different tattoo designs. He wanted to come up with a symbol he considered "suitably dystopian" before using permanent marker to draw it on Connor's and Ryan's faces.)

"Talent?" Mom echoed, gazing around the room at the bricks scattered out from a central blast point.

She looked like she wanted to say something else, but Deven suddenly raised his arm and shouted "DUUUUUDE!"

Mom retreated back upstairs in a hurry, but Ryan suggested we quit practicing anyway.

"We don't want to lose our edge," he said.

On Talent Show day, Mr. Maguire borrowed Tina's truck to haul our load of bricks to the school. Then he helped us stack them under the stage in the lunchroom.

"I wish you could stick around and hear our act," said Connor.

"Um, yeah," said Mr. Maguire. "You know I think Random Noise is cool," he said a little too heartily. "Too bad I have to teach a class," he added, moving quickly toward the exit.

"Good luck, Dudes," he called.

I watched him slide out of the lunchroom, ducking his head as he passed the office. Weird.

"Duuuuude!" Deven hooted, raising the arm of the monster he'd made out of his grandmother's Halloween scarecrow. He had painted some red cardboard claws for its gloved hands, covered its smiling autumn face with a vampire mask, and dressed it in his sister's fake fur coat.

Meanwhile, Nate was drawing UPC stripes on Connor's forehead with a marker. "Don't move so much or it will smudge," he said.

"I wish you could smash us with real guitars," Connor was saying. "But I guess that would be too expensive." We had made cardboard guitars instead, and painted them with swirly paint like the ones Random Noise used.

That morning we had painted our hair too. Nate and I had the longest hair (and Deven had his wig) so the three of us got to be rockers. Ryan and Connor were the guards. (They were the closest we had to bald, since their mom always gave them buzz cuts with her clippers at home.)

"I signed us up to perform last," said Ryan.

"That way our coolness will be fresh in the audience's mind when it's time to judge."

What with Ms Larkey's monetary encouragement, a lot of kids had signed up. It looked like the talent show was going to take all day. My stomach was already doing flip-flops. I wasn't looking forward to waiting through eighteen other groups.

The lunchroom tables had been pushed back so that there was room for most of the kids to sit on folding chairs. But the Dudes didn't have to worry about finding seats together. The talent show contestants all sat on the floor down front.

"Hi Tyler!" called Jayden, and the whole row of kindergarteners waved and said, "Duuuuude!"

I waved sheepishly and hoped that they weren't planning to rush the stage during the Dudes' performance.

Just then, Ms Larkey leaned over the music stand and spoke into the clip-on microphone, sending her sing-song voice booming around the lunchroom. "Welcome to the Sherwood School Talent Show!" she said. "Remember that performing is a delight for both audience and performer. So please give your attention to each group."

Ms Larkey left the stage.

The audience cheered.

The curtain opened to reveal an empty plat-form.

The audience cheered again. Everybody was probably happy to be missing class, but still, it was a great intro for the first group which was a bunch of second grade boys.

They climbed up onstage carrying real instruments—a clarinet, a drum, and two of those shaker things with the bells on them.

They nodded to Ms Larkey, who was stand-ing by the stairs.

She looked down at her computer. There was a restless pause while Ms Larkey searched and finally clicked on something.

Then the lunchroom filled with the sound of a hooted battle cry—followed by every kid in the school cheering and hooting back.

The dudes looked at each other.

"Oh no!" I said.

But Ryan didn't look worried. "No biggie,

guys. Just wait," he said.

We waited and watched while "Rock Down the Walls"—our song—played all the way through.

The audience cheered and clapped along.

"They do seem to like our choice of song," whispered Nate hopefully.

I told myself the guys on stage weren't near as cool as we were going to be. They shuffled around, pretending to play their instruments, which weren't even the ones on the recording. With wide eyes and pale faces, they looked stage-struck too.

"No competition, Dudes," Ryan assured us. "Don't worry."

But my confidence fell when the next group also used "Rock Down the Walls". This time it was a bunch of girls doing exercises to the music.

That was followed by a group that bounced balls to the rhythm of "Rock Down the Walls", then a gymnast who did flips to it. One group even dressed up as silver robots—I don't know what that was about, but they were playing our song.

I tried not to worry. But I was starting to

notice how many kids around us had either colored hair or smudges on their foreheads.

One boy actually *played* "Rock Down the Walls" on the violin. It was kind of squeaky, but at least he had talent, which is more than I can say for the girls who came out dressed in costumes from Vampire Musical but sang "Rock Down the Walls" instead of "My Bleeding Love".

Teresa led a troop of girls dressed in pink ballet shoes and tutus. Even Random Noise couldn't make that look less goofy. Meanwhile, I had noticed that, with each performance, the audience was getting quieter. Kids were slouching in their seats or napping on each other's shoulders. I even saw some of them doing homework! This was a crisis. And the Dudes were the last group.

"Nobody else *acted out* the video," Ryan reminded us as we hurried behind the curtain to stack bricks. "Are you with me?"

I wanted to crawl under the stage where the bricks had been, but I said, "Dudes aren't quitters."

Ryan grinned. "Right. Do it just like we practiced," he said.

Through the curtain, I could hear the audience getting restless and the teachers shushing them.

I looked around at Nate. "Dude! Where's your guitar?"

"Oh! Right," said Nate, scrambling under the stage to get it.

As soon as he was ready, we began. We had one difference right off the bat. We had cut our copy of the song so that the battle cry didn't play. Instead, right before the music started, Deven yelled out his own version of the battle cry:

"DUUUUDE!"

Unfortunately, there wasn't much response other than a soft groan from the audience and the shrieks of five kindergarteners.

Ryan nodded to Ms Larkey to start the mp3 Nate had given her.

She squinted at her screen and hit a button.

The curtain opened.

The guards, Ryan and Connor, started shoving me, Nate, and Deven onto the stage.

And out of the speakers blared:

"When you play or sing at school,
Rhythm is the golden rule..."

The audience was silent. The sweet tinkle of a xylophone echoed around the lunchroom along with Ms Larkey's sugary voice.

I realized she must have clicked on the wrong music just as Ryan gave me another shove.

"Just go with it," he hissed, pushing me toward the maze.

We did everything the way we'd practiced it—what else could we do?—but to Ms Larkey's music!

Actually, the song fit surprisingly well. *"Quarter notes get just one beat..."* the speakers warbled as Nate beat Ryan over the head with his guitar.

I impaled Connor's stomach with a drumstick while, *"Whole note with his belly round, fills the measure with his sound,"* echoed around the lunchroom.

Of course, we made sure to stab and slice

in rhythm. It *is* the "golden rule" after all. Our fight was allegro with staccato punches. (If you don't know what that means, you'd better learn the Rhythm Song!)

Pretty soon, the guards and the monster were feeling some *tremolos.* And the whole time, Ms Larkey's voice trilled sweetly about happy half notes and eager eighths.

I was so nervous it took me a while to realize that the audience was *loving* it. In fact, they were singing along! Maybe it was because we were the first group all day that hadn't played "Rock Down the Walls". Or maybe it was because there wasn't a kid in the school that didn't want to kick a brick wall when he heard the Rhythm Song.

By the time the sixteenth note sped *"up the scale and tumbled down",* Deven and Nate and I had sent the walls tumbling too. The audience was clapping and cheering. The teachers were laughing. And Ms Larkey had extra dimples on her rosy cheeks.

The fight ended with the walls demolished, the monster smashed, and the guards and band members strewn around the stage like corpses. Deven was the last man standing.

As the final verse of the Rhythm Song came to a close, he raised his guitar over his head, shouted, "DUUUUUDE!" hoarsely, clutched his heart, and fell backward into the rubble.

It was totally moving.

I saw the audience leap to its feet as the curtain swished closed. The sound of cheers was deafening.

The dudes got 25,000 Coconut Bucks for winning the Talent Show on top of the 500 we each got for entering.

But, best of all, we were celebrities. After that, the kindergarteners weren't the only ones who greeted us in the hall by shouting "DUUUUUDE!"

The Dudes on the Bus

Deven had taken his student council-y duties seriously all year. He had argued with Teresa at every meeting. He had suggested a whole party-mix of songs to the lunchroom music committee (which was, unfortunately, comprised of a bunch of girls). He had even delivered on *Teresa's* promise of an inspirational message in the morning announcements.

But, planning some fun into the fifth-grade field trip was the reason he was elected. When it came time to select a destination, Deven attended the first meeting with a mandate from the people and a site proposal. Unfortunately, for some reason, Speed Mountain—home of the fastest roller coaster on two continents—was not considered educational enough.

"Ms Grieber didn't believe me when I told

her we could learn about centrisigal force by riding the Super Looper," Deven complained.

"It's centrifugal force," Nate corrected him.

"So what's the field trip going to be?" Ryan demanded.

"It's a total scam," complained Deven. "Ms Grieber already had the choices planned. She said we have to choose between the state capitol and Fort Cat Soup."

We all stared.

"I believe he means Fort Clatsop," Nate supplied. "It was the winter camp of Lewis and Clark on their journey with the Corp of Discovery."

"Yeah. Those are the guys!" said Deven.

"Hey! A fort sounds pretty cool," said Ryan.

"Don't worry," Deven assured him. "I'm gonna be all over the fort trip in the next meeting. I already made up a list of supplies for each kid to bring."

He handed over the list which Ryan read out loud:

Provisions

- ◇ Beef jerky—("Because it's historical," Deven explained.)
- ◇ Fruit leather—("Which can also be used as bandages.")
- ◇ Wacky taffy—("Because the fruit flavor lasts a loooooong time!—and, besides, no one wants to eat cat soup, right?")

<u>Equipment</u>
- ◇ Water gun—rifle style.
- ◇ Water pistol—for backup.
- ◇ Extra water—for ammunition.
- ◇ Rubber chicken

"I figure we'll want to re-enact the whole battle of Lewis and Clark," Deven declared.

"Lewis and Clark weren't enemies," Nate pointed out.

"Then why did they build a fort?" Deven wanted to know.

No one asked about the rubber chicken, so Ryan kept reading.

<u>Clothing</u>
- ◊ Army Helmet
- ◊ Stick-on mustaches
- ◊ Camo undershorts

"I might wear my flaming fajita shorts instead," Deven admitted. But it was not to be.

At the next meeting, it only took Teresa two minutes to explain how a visit to the state capitol would go along with everything the fifth graders had learned this year about democracy and government. (I told you she was crazy persuasive.)

"We could see the legislature in session and maybe even meet the governor," Teresa had said.

And Ms Grieber forgot all about the water guns and army helmets...or tried to.

Good morning students. The fifth-grade field trip to the state capitol is today.

In other news: Due to disturbing effects on the food service staff, the music of Troy Diamond is hereby banned from the lunchroom until further notice.

Today's inspirational message is: Troy may be a diamond, but silence is golden!

You may now return to your regularly scheduled classes—all except fifth-graders! Woo-hoo! So long, suckers!

The fifth-grade field trip was a big deal. Every fifth-grader, thanks to Ms Larkey (and the Dudes), had paid 1000 Bucks to go on it, after all.

And, lucky for us, Teresa believes in doing things right. (I admit it, she can be cool some-times—and, like I said, persuasive.) There would be no rattle-trap school buses for us. Nope, the Dudes (and the rest of the fifth-graders) would be traveling in style. Teresa had convinced Ms Grie-ber to hire real tour buses by pointing out that they were modern, safe, low-emissions vehicles and would provide a more comfortable ride.

For once, the teachers were on the right side of the debate. Ms Finch was enthusiastic about saving the planet. Mrs. Hancock was pleased that the buses had their own bathrooms and thus would save scheduling time for bathroom stops. And

Mr. Isaac said the larger tour buses would provide room for more chaperones. (He seemed more worried than excited about the trip. I don't know what he thought might happen, but I've noticed that teachers can think of way more bad possibilities than Dudes can.)

Maybe that's why the teachers got completely obsessed with this idea of "appropriate clothing". As if the governor was going to throw us out of the state for being unkempt.

"Remember, you'll be entering the workplace of our state's leaders," squeaked Ms Finch, eyeing Connor's "A zombie ate the dog who ate my homework!" t-shirt.

"You'll stand taller and look sharper if you care about how other people see you," Mrs. Hancock said, frowning at Ryan's Random Noise t-shirt.

"Don't use your body as a billboard," said Mr. Isaak as he tried to avoid catching sight of Troy Diamond's giant face on the front of Teresa's dress.

Anyway, the teachers eventually sent home a note to our parents, which is why, on the day of the field trip, Ryan and Connor showed up at school wearing plaid shirts—you know the kind with buttons down the front and little pockets over the chest. Most of the other guys were dressed the same—including Nate and me—only mine had stripes and Nate's was plain blue.

Deven wore his suit coat again. This time he had a red tie to match his pocket handkerchief. "And I went with my red hot chili pepper underwear," he informed us, (which was more than I needed to know.)

His dad and his grandmother had volunteered as chaperones.

"The only reason my whole family didn't come," Deven said, "is because Mom is in the middle of a murder trial, and Shaila thinks field trips are lame."

As soon as the bell rang, the three fifth-grade teachers walked their classes out to the front of the school where we could hear the buses idling. They were two tall boxes in glossy black and silver paint. Through the tinted windows we could see plush, high-backed seats and video monitors mounted to the ceiling.

As we halted at the curb, Ryan passed the word: "Okay, Dudes. Get ready for Operation Seat Scramble."

But, before we could act, the teachers got in a huddle of their own, after which Mr. Isaak made an announcement:

"Fifth graders should line up with their friends and enter the buses beside the people with whom they wish to sit!"

We were stunned. And relieved.

Ryan gave Mr. Isaak the nod as the Dudes entered the first bus. "I'm impressed," he told me. "The teachers actually learned something this year."

As I climbed the stairs I caught sight of something I recognized in the pocket beside the driver's seat. Along with the folded city maps was a stash of comic books—the kind my brother likes.

It surprised me because the driver was an old guy with wrinkles and gray hair which was slicked back in a long, braided pony-tail. Dark glasses sat atop his head. He didn't look at anyone as we passed, just sat there with his hands on the wheel and a bored expression.

The Dudes took the five seats at the back, of course. By the time I got back there, Ryan already had the window down. "Our bus can beat your bus!" he yelled to the kids on the other bus.

Some of them were yelling back or making faces, although I could see that Teresa was turned away from her window, chattering excitedly to a bunch of girls. At least she wasn't wearing anyone's face today (except her own, of course).

Finally, Mr. Isaak gave the nod. The bus driver flipped his sunglasses down, and the bus started to move.

At that moment, I felt sorry for all the kids who weren't fifth-graders. It would suck to be stuck in class today.

"Whoa!" we hollered as the bus made the turn out of the parking lot.

I saw the bus driver check that big mirror over his head in time to see the Dudes lunging to the side like actors whose space ship has just hit an asteroid.

"Whoa!" we shouted again, lunging the other way as the bus rounded another corner.

By the third block, we had all the kids shrieking on the turns and pretending to fall out of their seats. Unfortunately, we were approaching the highway, and there would be no more turns for the next hour and a half.

"Too bad," said Ryan. "Dad said, one time this bus full of big football players rocked back and forth so hard they turned the bus over!"

"That would be awesome!" said Connor.

Nate and Deven and I just laughed as the bus started up the on-ramp.

"Chug-chug-chug!" chanted the Dudes as the bus accelerated.

"I think I can, I think I can!" yelled Ryan.

Was it my imagination, or did the bus driver crack a faint smile behind his sunglasses?

I guess I'll never know, because just then Mr. Isaak stood up and held a microphone to his mouth. "Quiet down so the driver can concentrate," he said, his voice booming over the speakers. Then he added ominously, "We don't want a *catastrophe* of any kind."

Nate settled back in his seat and unzipped his backpack.

"Dad loaned me his old phone," he said, taking out a smart phone and a cord which he plugged into the charging port on the seat arm. "The amenities are very convenient," Nate added. He began pulling various pieces of electronics out of his pack.

"How's the spy robot coming along?" I asked.

"I am attempting to develop a wireless connection between the robot's camera eye and my dad's video app. This trip should give me time to work on it," he said happily.

The rest of the kids weren't as excited about the drive time—especially after we hit a one-lane construction zone and the buses slowed down to forty miles an hour.

"I hope this doesn't make us late," worried Mrs. Hancock.

"Turn on the video!" somebody yelled.

Obligingly, the driver flicked on the monitors that were spaced at intervals around the ceiling.

The Dudes cheered, hoping for the Rock Down the Walls video or maybe the latest episode of **Ninja Tempest**. Instead, a cheerful cartoon head appeared, giving an introduction to the Microsoft Campus—in Korean, I think. Guess this bus company doesn't do a lot of school trips.

As far as I know, none of the kids in our fifth grade speaks Korean, and we weren't going to Microsoft anyway, but the bus driver left it on, and pretty soon things quieted down as kids gave in to the chirpy voice and the hypnotic effect of the glowing screens.

Now we could hear the murmur of adult voices from the six parent chaperones sitting at the front of the bus. The teachers were sitting between us and the parents. My guess is, they didn't want the chaperones to be disturbed by seeing their kids in field trip mode. But, by peering around Mrs. Hancock's poufy hairdo, I could see Nate's mom talking to Deven's grandmother.

They seemed to have really hit it off after Lunch Buddy day. That shouldn't have been a surprise. The frightening quality of the cheesy bread-sticks is a great conversation starter!

Mr. Singh was there too. He was staring at his phone.

"I must find an app to perfect my putting," said Deven in a perfect imitation of his father. "Maybe I will get a chance to play a round with the governor."

Ryan and Connor and I laughed, while Nate ignored everything but his robot program.

Seeing he had an audience, Deven pulled a fake mustache out of his pocket and stood up in the aisle, doing an impression that was either Hitler or a robot ski jumper.

And Deven wasn't the only one who had brought items from his list of field trip supplies. As an overpowering aroma of watermelon flooded the back of the bus, I looked over to see Connor clutching a gallon bag of various candies and chewing like he had the rubber chicken in his mouth.

"Want some?" he said, his mouth gaping to show a pink and green wad of wacky taffy. The color of his drool wasn't appetizing.

I grabbed a fruity tooter instead and tried playing Rock Down the Walls with it.

"Hey! You've got Tongue Zapperz!" said Deven, pointing to the bag. "I love that commercial." He proceeded to act out the scene we all knew so well in which Frankenstein's bolts get zapped by lightning and he sticks his electrified tongue out to show the candy.

"Zapperz: They'll give you a charge!" said Deven, repeating the tag-line and the Zapperz tongue face.

Predictably, Connor cracked up, spewing fruit-flavored spit and shooting his wad of taffy three feet before it landed in Ryan's shirt pocket.

"Awesome, Dude! How'd you do that?" said Deven.

But Ryan pulled out the pink and green wad and tried to decorate Connor's face with it. Connor ducked, but the candy stuck in his hair, making a pink and green lump on the side of his otherwise neat buzz cut.

Just then, the bus slowed down as we left the highway. The video cut off, rousing the students from their dazed condition.

"Be prepared to get off the bus in five minutes," announced Mrs. Hancock over the loudspeaker.

Nate put his robot pieces in the backpack and zipped it. It was only then that he looked up and saw the lump in Connor's hair. "Maybe you should try to get that out," he suggested.

Connor nodded and loped toward the bathroom, which was down a little flight of stairs in the middle of the bus.

Meanwhile, the bus pulled up right in front of the capitol building and stopped at the curb.

Kids stood up and jammed the aisle, but Mr. Isaak didn't let anyone off until he'd gotten a walkie-talkie from the bus driver and given last minute instructions to the teachers and chaperones.

"We don't want anyone to get lost," he said.

The walkie-talkie reminded me, and I turned to Nate.

"Hey, don't forget your dad's phone," I said.

"Oh right!" said Nate, hastily unplugging the charger and putting it and the phone in his pocket.

The Dudes followed the rest of the kids off the bus and onto the sidewalk, where we all stood staring up at the wide steps and the huge dome of the capitol building.

It wasn't until the bus had pulled away, that the Dudes realized one of our number was missing!

 # *Dudes Take the State*

"We just got here," complained Mr. Isaak. "How could anyone be lost?"

"Who is missing?" inquired Mr. Singh.

"Connor Maguire," the teacher answered.

"Oh," said Mr. Singh with a nod that suggested approval for losing Connor so quickly.

"He was in the bathroom," I explained. "He's probably still on the bus."

With a sigh, Mr. Isaak pulled out his walkie-talkie and called the bus driver.

"I'm caught in traffic," said the voice from the speaker. "I'll circle back around, but it will be a few minutes."

"Fine," said Mr. Isaak resignedly. "I'll wait for Connor. The rest of you follow Mrs. Hancock and Ms Finch into the legislative session before they recess."

"I didn't know they got recess here!" said Deven as we clomped up the steps.

Inside the capitol building, we had to pass through metal detectors. Lots of kids worried about their braces, but no alarms went off—even for Deven. (I guess there's no metal in a rubber chicken.)

Nate had to wait for his backpack to be hand-searched. The security guy didn't even blink at the robot parts.

"We don't worry too much about school groups being a danger," he said naively, waving us through. "Don't forget your bag, son," he added.

"Oh, right!" said Nate, running back for his backpack and then rejoining the line.

The teachers made a lot of noise shushing us as we stomped up one flight of stairs and then down some others to file into several rows of squeaky seats in the legislative chamber.

We were in a balcony overlooking a big room full of desks. The legislators below weren't doing much, as far as I could tell—just sitting around pretending to listen while someone else talked.

No wonder they needed recess. It looked a lot like school.

Mr. Singh wasn't looking at his phone now. He leaned over from the row behind the Dudes to point out the legislator from our district.

"That could be you someday," he whispered to Deven.

I watched our State Representative sit unmoving at her desk. It was hard to imagine Deven sitting still that long. Her legs were crossed, her face tilted down. I started to wonder if she was actually asleep. But, when it was her turn to vote, she suddenly called out "Aye!"

The other representatives called out "Aye" or "Nay" on their turns. Then everybody stood up, took their briefcases, and left the room. I guessed it was time for lunch.

Mrs. Hancock looked at her watch. "Let's move, people!" she called, hustling us out of the gallery and back down the stairs. At least we didn't have to go through the metal detectors on the way out.

Soon we were back out on the front steps

where Connor and Mr. Isaak met us carrying two big bags of sack lunches.

"The bus driver is actually a cool guy," Connor told us over sandwiches in the park.

"He looks kind of old," I said.

"Yeah. He says he can't afford to retire," Connor explained. "It's boring driving foreign tourists around town, but he gets to read comics on his break." Connor looked like he was considering the idea as a possible future career.

"He didn't give me a hard time for getting left behind," he said, "but I felt bad for making him miss some comic time so I gave him my candy bag."

"Speaking of candy, you still have pink and green in your hair," I pointed out.

"Really?" said Connor, patting his head.

Ryan laughed. "We'll have to shave your head, little brother," he predicted.

But Nate disagreed. "Since taffy is made mostly of sugar, it should dissolve in water," he explained.

Connor shrugged and opened his water

bottle. He leaned sideways, trying to pour it on the taffy, but, unfortunately, some went in his ear. Connor shook his head violently, splattering Mr. Isaak as he walked up to collect our trash.

"Let me advise students," the teacher announced wearily, "to please use only your *mouths* for drinking."

"It's almost time for our visit to the Governor's office," said Mrs. Hancock. "Trash your lunches, students. We're moving on!"

And we did: back through the metal detectors and down a hallway to a wide door that had the governor's name on it.

He wasn't there, of course. A young woman met us at the door and handed out campaign bumper stickers. Then she guided us inside and told us about the picture on the carpet which was the State Seal.

We all looked at the carpet.

Then the guide pointed to the big wooden desk. "This is where the governor does his work," she said, "signing bills approved by the legislature, giving press conferences, receiving reports on everything that happens in the state."

We all looked at the desk. I wondered if the governor had ever gotten reports on anything the Dudes had done.

"Sometimes the governor uses this phone to make and receive calls with the President of the United States!" said the guide.

We all stared at the phone.

"Doesn't he know how to skype?" Nate asked.

"Yes. Yes, of course he does," said the guide quickly. "The governor is very up to date."

"Where is he?" Ryan asked.

The guide opened her mouth, but, before she could answer, the big door opened and five men came in. Four of them were security guards, and one of them was the governor himself. I could tell because he had the same bushy mustache as in his picture on the bumper sticker.

He looked surprised to find his office so full of kids, but he quickly smiled and made the best of it.

"Well, boys and girls, teachers and parents,"

he said, looking around. "I'm afraid my security folks have decided to lock down the building for a few minutes—for our safety, of course."

The kids all started whispering. Getting caught in a lock down was way more exciting than looking at the carpet. But the teachers and parents looked concerned.

"It's probably nothing," the governor assured them. "These things happen a couple of times a week. Usually it turns out someone left some personal belongings in the gallery."

I looked at Nate whose eyes widened as he shrugged his empty shoulders.

The governor sported a cheerful grin beneath his mustache. "I guess we're stuck together until security gives us the green light," he said.

"What's going to happen to the backpack...I mean whatever personal item was left?" asked Nate carefully.

"Security has to check it out..." the governor began.

"To see if it's a bomb?" prompted Ryan.

"Now, I doubt it's anything like that," said

the governor with a strained chuckle. He looked around for a way to change the subject.

"While we're waiting, why don't we let one of these fine young people sit in my chair?" he suggested. He laid a hand on Deven's shoulder, saying, "You look like you're dressed for the job."

It was true. The governor also had a navy jacket and a red tie. He even had a red pocket scarf.

Luckily, Deven didn't say anything about his underwear. He just grinned and went behind the desk. He sat in the big chair and swung it around to face the window. When he turned around again, Deven was wearing a bushy mustache just like the governor's.

Mr. Singh flinched.

The governor's eyes widened, but he didn't say anything. I was getting the impression he was good with surprises—it was part of the job, I guess.

"Does anyone have any questions?" asked the governor.

"Have you ever shot anybody with that gun?" Ryan asked the security guard.

The guard gave him a steely look and answered, "Not yet."

The governor seemed anxious to change the subject again. His mustache twitched. He sniffed the air and took a step closer to Connor.

"Do I smell watermelon?" he asked.

Suddenly a strident voice answered: "Not on their school lunch trays!"

I saw the security guards tense up as Deven's grandmother strode toward the governor, her sari swinging. "Since we are here," Nani said boldly, "we should take the opportunity to discuss this issue."

The governor smiled and opened his mouth, but Nate's mom spoke before he could.

"She's right, sir," said Mrs. Howe, stepping up beside Deven's grandmother. "The children get very little fresh produce at school. The cooked entrees are full of fat and salt. And I heard they even had *pudding* during their standardized testing," she said indignantly.

Deven's grandmother nodded. "With so many fruits and vegetables grown right here in our state, it is a crime that we don't use them for the good of our school children," she said, crossing her arms.

"Way to go, Nani!" called Deven from behind the governor's desk.

"My son-in-law is a doctor," Nani went on, gesturing to Mr. Singh. "He can attest to the effect that nutrition has on the developing bodies of children."

Mr. Singh, who'd been staring at her with an open mouth, closed it again and then cleared his throat. "Uh, yes. That's right," he stumbled. "As a radiologist, I haven't studied the matter personally, but..."

That's when Deven pounded his fist on the desk for attention, accidentally dislodging one side of his mustache in the process.

"Okay, citizens, we all know how this debate should be settled," he declared. Then he turned to the governor. "Do you have any rocks in here?" Deven asked.

The governor's mustache twitched again. "Rocks?" he asked.

"Not for throwing," Connor assured him.

That's when Ms Finch stepped forward and told the governor how the students had been learning the Greek method of democracy.

"I'm impressed," said the governor when she had finished. "And you students should be impressed too with the caliber of teachers you have at...what was the name of your school?"

"Sherwood Elementary fifth-grade, sir," chirped Ms Finch proudly.

"Well, it sounds like you fifth-graders are ready to take over from me any day!" said the governor with a chuckle.

Then he turned back to Deven and said, "With your approval, maybe we can settle this matter with raised hands."

Deven grinned. "All in favor of healthy school lunches, say 'Aye!'" he shouted.

"Aye!" said the governor, raising his hand and smiling at Nate's mom and Nani who raised their hands gladly along with the class and Mr. Singh and the teachers. Under Nani's stare, even the security guards raised their hands.

Deven pounded the desk again. "The ayes have it!" he announced.

For once, Mr. Singh looked at his son with pride.

Then Deven's mustache fell off.

Security didn't return Nate's backpack. Luckily, his dad's phone was in his pocket. Once we were back on the bus, he was able to use it to replay the last images the robot saw:

First there was the scared face of a young security officer, his eyes widening as he unzipped a backpack full of electronic parts.

Next came a squirt of water.

Then static.

"Their explosive disposal procedure probably destroyed the robot itself," Nate lamented. "But at least the telemetry feed worked!" he added. "I can rebuild it after I save up for more parts."

"Maybe you should make a robot that looks less like a bomb," I suggested.

Nate nodded.

The buses were on the highway now. We were coming up to the one-lane construction zone that had slowed us down on the way to the capitol.

Suddenly we felt a lurch and heard the engine rev. The Dudes rushed to the windows to see our bus surge forward and move into the left lane to pass the other bus.

Ryan's eyes gleamed, and he started chanting, "Race! Race! Race!"

Sure enough, we were starting to gain on the other bus. As we pulled ahead, I could see our bus driver hunched over the wheel like a maniac and taking swift glances to measure our progress. He really was racing!

We took the lead just in time to beat the other bus into the one-lane construction zone, which meant we would be ahead of them all the way back to Sherwood Heights.

And, just as we passed the other bus, our driver turned his head to look, and I could swear he was making the Zapperz tongue face!

Dudes Bid Up

The last day of school was finally here: Our last day to be fifth-graders. Our last day to rule the school. And our last day to wait for the Elephant Gun.

Nate and Deven and I were standing at the fifth-grade door when Mr. Maguire drove up in his girlfriend's truck. As Ryan and Connor hopped out of the cab, Mr. Maguire yelled out the open window: "Good luck at the auction!"

"Dad's psyched about the Elephant Gun," Ryan told us as he and Connor joined the line. "He wanted to get us one when they first came out, but Connor and I were babies, and Mom made him buy diapers instead. He's gonna come by your house after school to see it."

"Fine by me," I said. But I hoped we weren't jinxing ourselves by making plans like that.

"I counted our money last night," Nate reported. "We have over 30,000 Coconut Bucks between us. Let's see. It's here somewhere..."

We all had a bad moment as Nate unzipped all the pockets of his (new) backpack. But, when he finally pulled out the wad of coconut cash, my worries melted away. It sure looked like more money than anybody else had.

Ryan slapped a hand over Deven's mouth before he could hoot. "Play it cool, Dudes!" he hissed. "Don't let anybody know how much money we have or that we're working together.

Nate split the money between us.

Ryan even advised us to sit with our classes for once, and bid on some small items so as not to call attention to what we were really interested in.

"A couple hundred here or there won't matter," he said. "But," Ryan looked around, then spoke in a whisper. "When the *you-know-what* comes up, let me handle it!"

When Mrs. Hancock's line entered the lunchroom, I could see all the stuff from Ms Grieber's closet laid out on two tables on the stage. It was less crowded and better lighted, but, basically it was the same as I remembered from Nate's video.

Ryan elbowed me in the ribs as we passed. Sure enough, there on the second table was the Elephant Gun in all its green and purple splendor. If all went well, by the end of school it would be ours.

Ryan and I averted our gaze and walked along casually. Behind us, in Mr. Isaak's line, I heard Deven screech, "LOOK AT THAT!...thing I'm not interested in," he finished awkwardly.

That wasn't so bad, I thought.

Unfortunately, Deven went on. "Nope! Won't be bidding high today!" he yelled in case anybody wasn't paying attention yet.

Luckily, Mr. Isaak, the auctioneer, banged his little wooden hammer on the music stand to get our attention. It made a sound like a cymbal, causing a bunch of girls to jump and Mr. Isaak to hold his head.

"Please come to order," said Mr. Isaak grimly, as he hunched over the microphone.

When the audience settled down, he gestured to the tables of displayed merchandise like he was pointing out frog livers in science class. "As you can see, there are many fine items for auction," he intoned, adding, "so we need to get this thing going or it will take all day."

Mr. Isaak unfolded a paper on the stand. "Please pay close attention to these rules," he said.

1. "There will be no shouting. You must raise your hand to make a bid.

2. "All bids are in Coconut Bucks. We do not accept cash, barter, or Pokemon cards.

3. "You must have enough Coconut Bucks here today to pay for your purchase."

At that moment, Ms Grieber motioned to him from the side of the platform.

Mr. Isaak walked over to her.

Ms Grieber whispered something in his ear.

Mr. Isaak nodded, returned to center stage, and announced:

4. "There will be no backsies."

I guess Ms Grieber didn't want to be loaded down with this stuff for her retirement.

At last the auction began. The first thing

on the auction block was a robot arm. It was made from a kit I'd seen advertised on TV. Only somebody had already done the kit, attaching all the gears and rubber bands to make it move when you use a joystick in the base.

Without a computerized brain or digital mapping, this robot arm was way too primitive for a kid like Nate. It was really more of a puppet than a robot—and only a piece of one at that. I was just wondering who would want such a thing when Mr. Isaak announced:

"Sold! To Deven Singh."

I turned around to look as Deven shuffled out of the row where he and Nate were sitting with Mr. Isaak's class and ran up to the stage.

When Mr. Isaak handed it to him, Deven raised the robot arm in the air, turned, and shouted "Duuuuude!"

The audience hooted back.

Mr. Isaak shook his head.

I could tell Deven was happy with his purchase. He used the robot arm to bid for and win the next item in the auction—a baseball cap.

Back in his seat, Deven used the robot arm to put the cap on his head—then to lift it off—then to put it back on again.

"This is going to be really useful!" he said.

Next Deven started giving robotic high-fives to me and Ryan and the other kids in Mrs. Hancock's class. I was beginning to see why the robot arm had gotten confiscated in the first place.

Onstage, Mr. Isaak seemed to be trying to ignore Deven and the behavior of his class in general. He pushed ahead with the auction.

Nate bought seventeen solar powered dancing monkeys that he said might come in handy for spare parts.

"Freedom!" yelled Deven, raising the robot hand in solidarity with the monkeys.

I bought somebody's lost Lego guy for Jayden (in case some day he wasn't too annoying and I felt like giving him something—or in case I needed to bribe him, whichever came first).

On my way back from the stage, I could see Deven using the robot hand to wave to Connor way back in Ms Finch's class. Meanwhile, in my row,

Ryan's gaze was focused on the stage, every muscle frozen with tension, vigilant in case Mr. Isaak suddenly skipped over to table two and the Elephant Gun.

At the moment, Mr. Isaak was selling a calculator watch, and the bids were going pretty high.

"I have one thousand Bucks," said Mr. Isaak.

"Wow. That's a lot of Bucks," Ryan commented.

"Do I hear two thousand?" asked Mr. Isaak. Then he nodded toward the back and said, "Two thousand. Good."

"Oooh," said the audience in appreciation.

"Who'd have thought two people wanted a calculator watch that badly?" I said.

"I'm bid three thousand," announced Mr. Isaak.

"And who has that much money to burn?" asked Ryan.

Ryan and I realized what was happening at the same moment. Before Deven could raise the robot arm (and the price!) again, we both turned and pounced on him, rattling the folding chairs as we lunged into the row behind us.

Ryan wrenched the robot arm out of Deven's hands, hissing, "Stop bidding, doofus, and let the other guy win!"

That's when Mr. Isaak drawled, "Sold! For four thousand Coconut Bucks to Connor Maguire."

I groaned, and Ryan went purple. Whether Connor had been competing against a robot or just waving to one, he now owned a calculator watch, and the Dudes were down four thousand Bucks!

Connor bounded up to the stage with a pleased look on his face. As he passed us, coming back with the watch, Ryan whispered, "Don't bid on anything else, guys. We've got to save our money!" Then Ryan put the robot arm under his seat and forbid Deven to wave to it.

To get to the Elephant Gun, we had to wait through the whole first table and part of the second. It was boring now that we couldn't bid.

Gina Bertrelli bought something called an add-a-bead necklace that she said was "vintage."

Sean Chang bought a package of Peeps he said was lost by his cousin in the spring of 2010. I guess that was vintage too.

Teresa bought a teeny-tiny sequined sombrero (probably for her Mexican Chihuahua). I knew Teresa must have some Bucks left, since she was the only girl who refused to buy Sushirasers from us.

There was the usual run of Matchbox cars and sparkle markers. There was even a musical toothbrush with Troy Diamond's face on it.

"What am I bid for this unusual piece of... personal hygiene memorabilia?" asked Mr. Isaak. But even the girls didn't want a used toothbrush that sings "Don't Brush Me Off." We were getting down to the last few items and the last of people's Coconut Bucks, too.

Teresa used her Bucks to buy that cardboard box we'd seen in Nate's video, which Mr. Isaak called "The Surprise Box". I figured it was filled with all the little things that wouldn't sell on their own. Maybe the jelly shoe was in there, along with probably a bunch of Sticky-Snot and little kids' toys.

At last, the moment came that the Dudes

had been waiting for all year:

"What am I bid for this harmless hunting toy?" asked Mr. Isaak, the irony heavy in his voice. (Guns aren't allowed in school, but I guess Ms Grieber thought up a clever name so she could get away with selling this one. Maybe Gina Bertrelli could have saved her phone from confiscation by calling it "a device for transmitting information".)

"It comes complete with three toy projectiles," Mr. Isaak announced dryly, displaying the oversized darts.

All over the lunchroom, I could feel the tension as guys recognized the Elephant Gun and begged each other for more Bucks to buy it. Some of them even thought of hurriedly banding together, but no one had many Bucks left after the field trip.

No one but the Dudes!

After all that worry, Ryan won the bidding easily with a couple thousand Bucks to spare. And when all five Dudes sauntered up on stage to claim our purchase, the audience hooted. We were the kings of cool!

After working so hard for them, it was almost a shame to toss the rest of the Coconut Bucks in the recycle bin. Of course, all their worth had depended on the Elephant Gun. That's what Nate calls a "gold standard". I saved one so I could attach a digital copy to the Chronicle of the Dudes—that's the Buck you saw back in chapter 2.

After school, we couldn't wait to try out the Elephant Gun. The spring was strong, all right. Connor tried to dry-fire it and the kickback nearly knocked him out of the treehouse!

"I'll design a gun mount," Nate promised.

In the meantime, Ryan braced himself against Connor, found his range, and fired.

Wow! Maybe it was the stronger spring or the heavier dart, but I had never seen one fly so far. The Elephant Dart flew across our yard, over Mrs. Kostenko's gazebo, and into Teresa's back yard where it sailed past the pink walls of her treehouse and thumped against the side of her house. If it ever came to war with Teresa, it looked like the

Dudes had superior firepower.

Of course, Teresa wasn't in the line of fire at the moment. I found out later that the surprise box she bought at the auction had all the Sushirasers the teachers had been confiscating from girls all year long! My guess is, as soon as school was out, Teresa called a gathering of Sushi-heads in order to trade up for a Dragon King and finally get that full Bento set.

Was she smart or just lucky? It's always hard to tell with Teresa.

Meanwhile, Ryan had Connor in the usual half-nelson when he noticed something unusual. He snatched the new/old calculator watch off Connor's wrist to get a better look at what was scratched on the side:

"Kevin Sean Maguire," said Connor, his eyes wide. "Those are Dad's initials!"

"This is Dad's watch!" said Ryan. "But how did it get in Ms Grieber's closet?"

"Wait 'til we tell him we have it!" said Connor.

But Mr. Maguire wasn't so happy to see that watch when he came over later. "I had hoped you'd never find out about this, boys," he told us.

He had climbed right up in the dojo with us to try the gun, which was pretty cool for a parent. And it was there that he told his story—a true story this time.

"See, back in school, I was so busy trying to be cool, that I almost flunked math," said Mr. Maguire, swinging his legs off the side of the top platform.

"My parents didn't know," he said, "and I thought I could solve the problem on my own. When my dad got me this watch, I tried to use it to cheat on a math test."

"Whoa," said Ryan, shocked.

Mr. Maguire picked at a hole in the knee of his jeans. "It gets worse," he said. "Ms Grieber was my math teacher. When she caught me, she took my watch. I was so embarrassed, that I just left it sitting in her closet," he admitted. "I guess that's where it's been all these years."

The Dudes were silent.

"What about your grade?" Nate finally asked.

Mr. Maguire looked up. "Ms Grieber gave me an F," he said. "She always was a mean old witch," he grumbled.

Then he sighed. "She also made me work hard until my grades came up. Come to think of it, I guess that's how I got my confidence in math."

"So it's Ms Grieber's fault you ended up a math professor!" said Ryan, outraged.

Mr. Maguire chuckled. "I guess you could put it that way," he said. "So let that be a lesson to you boys!" he added like he suddenly remembered he was a parent. Then he picked up the Elephant Gun.

"Don't worry, Dad," said Connor. "I'll only use this watch for good, not evil."

Thinking back, I realized the watch and the cheating incident explained why Mr. Maguire kept sneaking off to avoid being seen by Ms Grieber—not that anyone would want to be seen by Ms Grieber if they could help it. I wondered what other stories might lurk behind the artifacts that used to be hidden in Ms Grieber's closet.

And, speaking of stories, I'm guessing there will be more to come from the Dudes. Now that we've taken over the state and ruled the school, we'll need to cut loose from all that responsibility and have some summer fun.

Don't worry. I'll keep you posted.

Don't miss the next exciting adventure of the Dudes...

Leave No Dude Behind!
It's gonna be a summer like no other. Luckily, the Dudes are prepared to take on:

- *Being Lost at Sea*
- *Earthquake!*
- *Bigfoot!*
- *A Robot Invasion!*
- *and Teresa's Chihuahua!*

Don't miss the mayhem in:

Summer of the Dudes

Coming soon to amazon.com

Tyler Reynolds has been entrusted with the awe-some duty of preserving the legend of the Dudes' epic adventures for all time. He lives with his Mom and Dad, two brothers, and a dog and spends his non-screen-time with his four best friends.

Check out his website at: **thedudeschronicles.com**

Emily Kay Johnson occasionally comes out of hiding to collaborate with Tyler on the dubious project of sharing the exploits of the Dudes with the world. She lives with her husband, sons, and cats in the Pacific Northwest, and she has her own logo.

You can reach her at **EmilyKayJohnson.com**

Made in the USA
Middletown, DE
26 December 2018